EDWARD'S CAT

THREE CATS, A MAGICAL LEGACY. AND A DOG.

MARIA P FRINO

Edward's Cat. Three Cats, a Magical Legacy. And a Dog.

Book 3

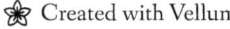 Created with Vellum

For everyone who encourages me to write
For my readers
I write for all of you

INTRODUCTION

A Brief History of *The Magicals*.

Jacaranda Trees are well known in Australia with the most common variety being *Jacaranda Mimosifolia*. Even though many Australians think of Jacarandas as being native to Australia, they are actually native to South America.

So, it is in South America that The Magical's Australian story begins. In 1800, the Rodriguez family sailed to Sydney, Australia. Santiago and Isabella along with their child, Lucas were invited to live in Sydney as Santiago's medical skills were required in this new territory. As a trained doctor, Santiago was able to help at Sydney's hospitals by training Australian doctors with his modern ways of medicating the population. One of which was the use of opium to treat oral conditions and toothache. This, along with his other skills, became valuable to the medical profession of Sydney.

The Rodriguez family found themselves in the top echelons of Sydney's society, living in a sprawling house not far from the hospitals and universities Santiago had to attend. Once the Rodriguez family became established, others from South America followed. Some were family, others were friends. They were all magicals.

Santiago did not need to change his last name to be part of Sydney's elite because of his good reputation, but some of the other South Americans he encouraged to emigrate, did. Santos became, Smith, Cabello became Cabel ... many names were changed to Anglo spelling. They wanted to fit into the Sydney high society quickly and progress to the status that was afforded to their friend, Santiago.

With the help of these overseas counterparts, the magicals set up the first Australian magical committee of whom Santiago was the head. He proceeded to appoint members of his family to positions within the committee and two of his good friends as well.

This secret society grew as Sydney grew. They were always wary of not exposing themselves to the non-magicals. Although, there was an incident in 1908 that nearly outed all of them.

As the economies of this new country prospered, so did Santiago and his family. They moved several times to newer and more affluent suburbs, one of which was Glenndale. The house in which Santiago would take his last breath is now a derelict house near the old industrial area of the suburb. This is still the headquarters for The Magicals.

ONE

Logan
A Swim at Dusk

I'M STARING out at the waves that are calming now it's dusk, they lap rather than rush the shore. Jack and I had gone for a late afternoon swim and are now sitting on our towels contemplating the year ahead, our last year of school. Thinking about it now, thirteen years have skidded by and we students are all wondering what the future will look like for us.

The beach is deserted, only a few surfers languishing out there chatting, there are no waves to speak of now. A few people walking their dogs, sticks and balls being chased. I enjoy being here at this time, with the sun lowering and changing the sky to colours of deep yellows and reds signalling another hot day tomorrow, it's peaceful. Summer is my favourite season.

"We start our final year tomorrow. Can you believe that?"

"Incredible, isn't it, Jack? Who knows what is ahead of us. A lot more free time, I hope."

"Do you think those bullies learned a lesson with the paralysing spell your dad placed on them? It would be nice not to have to deal with them this year, we're going to be busy with our HSC."

"They probably didn't, as much as I hate to say that. Dad went back to put a memory spell on them before they came out of the paralysing one, how much of their doomed futures do you think they will remember?"

"Right, of course. Your dad couldn't leave it that they remember him putting a spell on them, but their futures on that magical screen looked awful – injuries, carnage and gaol time."

"Oh they were certainly scared, fear tracked through all four of them. But their stupidity will get in the way of them doing any better. Like you, I hope they stay out of our lives this year."

Jack has his hands on his knees while staring out to sea. He nods silently and we spend the next few minutes with our own thoughts.

DINNER IS ready when I arrive home, my parents are sitting at the table. "Yours is in the oven, ready for you after you shower."

I take in the smell of the roast chicken and rush upstairs, a quick shower is needed because I'm starving after that swim. While in the shower, my thoughts go to the night of the paralysing spell, if it wasn't for our fathers, Edward and Noel, coming to our rescue, we would probably have ended up in hospital. Donovan and Parker were pissed we had a hand in them being locked up and they are now on house arrest, so will be out for revenge. How convenient the bracelets on their ankles were not out of range, our local park is a safe distance from their homes, their bracelets won't go off.

Back in the kitchen, I place my dinner on the table. "Yum, looks good, Mum." My parents were finishing off their dinner.

"Enjoy. Could you please finish tidying up, we need to go to the Alliance house for a few hours."

"Sure, Mum. Not anything serious, I hope."

Dad stands up taking his plate to the sink. Scraping the scraps into the bin and placing his plate in the dishwasher, he turns and says, "No, we need to discuss and clear up a few things so we're ready when we go back for this year's meetings."

I simply nod, with my dad being part of the magical society's committee, he spends a lot of time doing things to ensure we magicals are safe and our secret isn't discovered by non-magicals. Dad has the power to transform into a ginger cat, I shapeshift into a Maine Coon and my mum can conjure things, good and bad. We are part of the A-Alliance Magical Society, a group of people who have magical powers and do good deeds. We're a smaller society in Australia, many overseas societies are twice the size of ours.

With the kitchen tidy, I sit on the lounge and browse to see what's on television. Nothing much, so I turn down the volume leaving it on some drama show and scroll through my phone. My school friends are all chatting how we're already going back to school tomorrow and moaning about the end of the six-week holidays, our longest period of time away from school each year.

I join the chat with some of the other Year 12 students. I want this year over so bad.

You're not the only one Aaron, I've had enough, need to move on with my life.

It's not long now.

Suppose so, Logan. How was your swim this afternoon?

Great. Water was perfect temperature, Jack joined me.

Yeah was sick. Best time to go, hardly anyone around.

Yep, it is, Jack. Such a refreshing thing to do at the end of a hot day. Summer is over in a month.

Yeah, cold weather heading our way. Aaron, you playing soccer again this year?

Of course, Manuel. Logan, you and me, we're all signing up for weekend soccer right?"

Yep.

Sure am.

The chat continues for hours, we talk about soccer, school and inevitably about the bullies. We all agree we want them to leave us alone but know they don't give up easily. Even with Donovan and Parker doing a short stint in gaol, there is every chance they will be angry with us and attack, possibly be even more brutal.

I hear the front door. Mum and dad see me in the lounge, "Hey, we're exhausted, see you in the morning."

"Sure, Dad. Sleep well you two."

My parents are hardworking and well respected in the community. I'm lucky they are cool with me doing as I please but then I don't do anything for them to worry about, other than maybe being hurt by bullies when I'm in my cat form. We animals know how to dodge them as we're quick and can scurry away from danger easily. Jack, Chloe and I can shapeshift, Jack into a Jack Russell, Chloe is a Ragdoll and I'm a Maine Coon. My father is a shapeshifter too, he is a ginger, Milly the Cat. This is a long story, but basically, my Aunt Milly was ill when she was young and passed away bestowing her powers as Milly the Cat to my Dad. This means Dad was not born a magical, he inherited her magical power. But we are all magicals and have the best interests of non-magicals, this is our superpower.

I do wonder how non-magicals would react if our secret ever was discovered, but given many people are sceptical about such things, somehow I don't see things going too well. For now, it's a secret and has been since ancient times.

TWO

Donovan
The Bullies' Revenge

I STOP in front of Parker's house and watch as he walks down the front path. He may not speak often but he has my back at all times. We are part of a gang now, having both left school. We did have another two dudes who helped us, Alex and Callum, but those wimps haven't been around much lately. I haven't seen them at one of our gang meetings for ... well, I can't remember the last time I saw them.

Parker and me head to our gang's headquarters. If you can call it that. The ramshackle tin shed in the old industrial area of Glenndale is hidden by thick privet, overgrown bush and jacaranda trees, which have flower buds starting to show. We enter via the rusted entrance and greet others already there. The gang, which doesn't have a name, is a muddle of young petty thieves and older career criminals. They number thirty at times, but twenty are active at the moment.

Cole, one of the older crims and head of this gang of bullies we have joined, is yelling at all of us to stop and listen. "Hey, you dickheads, shut up cause I need to tell you what we're doing next. After the situation where some weird crap, probably magic but who the-F- knows, froze us to the spot at the park, we need to show those geeks we're not to be messed with. And if there is magic happening, we need to deal with it."

He waits until the cheering and clapping subsides. "Especially you young shits who have joined us from school, listen up. We need to do somethin' big to show them who's boss. Glenndale isn't big enough to have more than one gang, the geeks need to know we're the bosses and they answer to us." He stops and fiddles with a battered leather bag he has thrown over his shoulder and produces a laptop. He fires it up and asks Maddox, me and Parker to gather behind him.

"Right, we're going to target a few convenience stores in succession, one near the shopping centre, one on the main drag, and the smaller one near the outlet centre. Not all at once, but a timed attack that will happen over two months. Maddox, you're in charge of the shopping centre one, Donovan you take the main drag, and Parker you work the outlet one. Each of you pick your teams, I want six in each and each team leader will work out a plan based on this one I am emailing you after this meeting. Take a quick look now and ask me questions later."

The three of us look at the plan Cole has formulated and we each nod in his direction. "Good, now this meeting is over, you three choose your people, organise times to meet and discuss your plan then pass it by me. No discussions about what we're planning outside of our group. We right now? Any questions?"

No one replies so Cole tells everyone to start getting organised and dates will be finalised once all plans have been approved. "The esky is in the usual spot, let's drink to showing those geeks and the people of Glenndale we're not to be messed with."

With a lot of chatter, the whole group moves towards the '*bar*' area as we select our team members. One person we choose is a bulk of a man named Hubert. When we were first introduced to him, we struggled not to laugh. "Yeah, go ahead, laugh," Hubert had said at the time, "me mam loved reading love stories, especially history ones, and she fell in love with the name Hubert. My bad luck, eh? Just call me Hub."

"Nah, it's ok, Hub" I replied, "we need your strength and your massive body to scare people, no one will care what your name is."

There is much back slapping and ideas thrown around for the next hour as we all become excited to be exacting revenge against those who dare to humiliate us. Me, I still want to target the geeks from school too. Even though we have left, they need to know we haven't gone soft, they will know we're still around and are a force, especially with the backing of this gang.

"Hey, Parker, time we go. We're meeting the girls." Parker looks towards me and nods. "Guys, we'll talk soon," I indicate to my three newest members.

They acknowledge me and Hub, who is an experienced serial criminal and probably our best asset, says, "Look forward to it, boss." I smile, I can't believe someone his age and of his standing, is calling me *boss*.

. . .

MILLER AND SCARLETT are already at the bowling alley. "Hey babe." I greet Miller by pulling her close to me kissing her with passion. She's mine and sometimes I have to pinch myself that a girl this beautiful wants me.

"Where you two been? We've been waiting."

"Chill, we had business to attend to. Do you wanna bowl or not?" I don't know why she's so pissed, we're only half an hour late.

"I'm not interested now. What about you, Scarlett?"

"Can take it or leave it? Whatever you guys decide."

"Alright then, I have an idea. My olds are out for the night, we can go back to my place and raid the booze cabinet." Neither me nor Parker has the money to move out yet, we both still live with our parents. My stepdad is a cool guy, he won't mind if we *borrow* some of his beers."

"Sounds good to me, better than a lame game of bowling. Let's go," answers Parker then he and the girls follow me back to my crapped-out Corolla, it's a rust bucket but still works, which is all I care about.

Arriving at my weatherboard home that is only ten minutes' drive, the front yard is a mass of rusted out cars, my stepdad sells car parts but never gets rid of the cars themselves. He owns this house, apparently he grew up here and never left. Me and my mum have lived here for the past ten years.

Entering into the hallway, I tell them to head to my room. "I'll get some beers and snacks. Meet you in there."

They're already settled in when I enter my room. Miller is sitting on my bed, Parker is seated in my gaming chair with Scarlett on his lap. They're enjoying passionate kisses, oblivious to anyone else in the room.

"Take a breath you two. Here," I joke as I hand them their beers. I place a bowl of chips and a few chocolate bars on the table. "That's it for snacks, but we have plenty to drink, so let's enjoy."

"Cheers," says Parker offering his bottle that we clink following his lead.

A few hours later we are happily drunk, Parker and Scarlett asleep on the floor and me and Miller enjoying each other. Her kisses are all over my body, I'm so pumped and ready for her.

She stretches and looks up at me when we're finished. She starts on at me again about us being late. "So, where were you guys?" She slurs slightly, but she's not as drunk as me.

I'm pissed off she won't let this go. "None of ya business. We were with the gang, that's all. Nothing to worry your pretty little head about." She's about to answer but I continue, "Don't start your shit about me not being in the gang, I'm happy there. I'm respected, so I ain't leaving just cause you don't like Cole."

She stands up and starts getting dressed. "I don't trust him, Donovan. Don't think you should either. And don't say 'pretty little head' again, it's demeaning. Now, you'd better get me home, it's late. Come on, Scarlett, wake up." Scarlett moans moving her hand to her yawning mouth.

I don't know what Miller is talking about because she is pretty, but I decide not to start an argument, she'll get on her soap box about women's rights. "Can't drive in this state, Parker should be ok, he's slept it off. Parks, get up and take the girls home."

Parker yawns, zips up his jeans and puts his t-shirt back on. "Yep, I'm ready for more sleep too, best get home. See you soon, Don."

I see them out the door and shut it after them. Bloody Miller talking shit about Cole, he's a good leader and I respect his leadership. I'm sure these next jobs we're going to do will make others respect Cole and our gang as a whole.

After taking a piss, I go back to my room exhausted. It's been a great day apart from Miller and her stupid comments.

THE THREE GROUPS are listening to Cole at another meeting. This time we have finalised what will happen at each convenience store. My group will target the one on the main street, in daylight, which I think is stupid but I don't say anything, Cole is the big boss, no one crosses him or answers back.

"Right, you're all set. Don't stuff this up and be gone before the police arrive, you know there are alarms at all of these stores. Go on, get outta here and practise what you've been told. And stick to the plan, don't put anyone in danger."

As Parks and me are walking to the car, I yell, "Hey guys, you too Hubs, how about a drink to talk about what we need to do. A type of rehearsal."

They head towards my car and I drive to The Arms, buying them a drink before I sit down. At this time of the day, the pub is empty so we're free to talk. Hubs is full of information about other heists he's done in the past, successful ones. I'm so pumped about doing this, being in a real gang is extra!

THREE

Logan
The Final School Year

I HEAD towards the convenience store after alighting from my school bus. My tap card needs topping up. The bell dings as I enter, the cool air hitting me in a flash. I decide to browse for a bit to take in the coolness. Grabbing a few chocolate bars and a large bag of chips, I head to the counter greeting the man behind it.

"$15.90 thanks."

"Oh, I almost forgot. Top this up please." The man proceeds to top up my tap card handing it back to me. He is about to speak when ...

There is an almighty bang near the entrance as a group bursts into the store. I stare in fear. Looking towards the guy handing me my change, I see the fear in his eyes too. He looks to be seeking a button under the counter.

Four youths covered with balaclavas, one holding a

cricket bat, rush the counter. The one holding the bat brandishes it at the man. "Don't you dare press that thing or this here bat will find your head. And this bag is to be filled with cigarettes, money and chocolates," says the main thug pointing to the thug who has suddenly appeared next to the man. He is holding a large striped bag used for storing clothes. "Now!" The other two thugs behind us are filling bags up through the aisles.

"And you, piss off." He's yelling at me. I look into his eyes, his voice sounding familiar. Donovan maybe? But when he lunges at me, I decide to cut my losses and leave.

I head out of the entrance and call Triple o shakily telling them the address and what's happening, then hang up because two of the thugs are already outside. "Hey you." I run around the corner and transform. One of them runs after me, this huge man who is bald and has a bushy beard tinged with red is beyond scary, he is massive.

As I saunter back towards him terrified he's going to stomp on me, he stops and looks around. He's probably wondering where the hell I disappeared to and maybe looking for the owner of this Maine Coon cat. I jump at his ankles and scratch as hard as I can. He screams with a bear-like roar as I run behind the bushes to transform.

The second thug is trying to find me, "Where's that cat?"

"How should I know? These scratches, look at them. They're stinging like hell."

"Who cares about your legs, help me find that cat."

"It's hard to walk ..."

"Jesus, Hub, you're hopeless."

I stay as still as I can behind the bushes so they won't find me. My body shakes, bile rises in my throat when I see both their legs in front of me. Then ... a ginger cat appears. My dad is here.

I watch as Milly the Cat, this is the animal my dad can shapeshift into, it's the power his twin sister had. She bestowed this power to him when she passed away at a young age. Jumping up onto one of the thugs, her teeth sink into his hand and then she scratches the bigger thug, the one I attacked, in the same spot I did. The raucous this causes from these two as they scream brings other people to the site, there is now an audience.

Dad joins me in the bushes and transforms.

"I'm glad you're here, Dad. But why ... how are you here?"

"I was driving home and saw the commotion. Something told me one of you could be in trouble, many of your group come here often. So I thought I'd see what was happening, and I was right, you're the one in trouble."

Suddenly, the other thugs burst out of the entrance to the store and run to a black car where there is someone in the driver's seat waiting for them. The thug with the hand wound runs to the car just as the car speeds off with a screech. The smell of tyres burning attacks our noses. The big thug is still standing near us, Dad and I are trying to stay calm.

The police arrive soon after the getaway car sped off and we breathe a little easier. I hear a police officer talking into a microphone, I recognise her voice. Dad and I walk towards her, I see she is handcuffing the thug I had attacked, he had been inspecting his wounds and didn't make it to the car. He glares at me and I try to stand my ground hoping on one sees how much I'm shaking with fear. I am trying to control it.

"Constable Jane Pathe, hello. Remember me, Logan Shipley. Can I help?"

She looks at me without recognition at first, then, "Oh yes, you helped us with the investigation into bullying and cyber-attacks. And this is your father." Dad holds out his hand and she shakes it. "No thanks Logan, but thanks for offering, I'm good here. Just escorting this man into the police car." She heads towards the car where another officer is holding the back door open. "I'll go and speak with the store owner, you watch him please." The other officer nods.

I wait around in case she needs to speak to me. I'm still deciding whether I tell her that I think it was Donovan holding the bat and threatening the store owner. But am I really sure it was him? What if it's someone else with a similar voice?

A few minutes later, Constable Pathe comes out of the store with the owner. "Is this the boy you were serving." The man nods. "Logan?" she asks trying to remember my name again. When I nod *yes*, she continues, "Do you think you can identify any of these youths?"

"Umm, I don't think so, they wore balaclavas and were all dressed in black." I had decided quickly enough not to mention Donovan until I was sure.

"Well, if you remember anything else, you know where to find me."

"Thanks, Constable Pathe, will do. Sorry I wasn't much help."

"I'll hear from you I hope. I'm glad no one has been hurt here." She says this as she heads to the police car with the other officer already in the driver's seat. They drive off.

Well no one except that bulk of a man. I snicker to myself so happy he didn't hurt me. I look towards the shop owner, "Are you ok? This is my father, by the way." He nods towards dad who acknowledges him.

"I'm ok now. What happened to those two thugs that followed you?"

"Well, it was the strangest thing. These two cats came out of nowhere and attacked them, the bigger one scratched the big guy's ankles and a ginger cat bit the hand of the other one."

"Really? Well we do have a few feral cats around here. I'm glad you're ok, sorry this happened while you were in my shop."

"We were lucky we weren't hurt and it's not your fault. I'm sure the police will find them, just a bunch of idiot kids, I think."

The man doesn't answer, he gives me his hand and we shake. He nods to dad and we watch him go inside to assess the damage, at least I assume that is what he will do.

"Well, this has been an eventful afternoon. Thanks for bringing Milly out Dad, she hasn't be around for a bit."

"No problem, Logan. She is semi-retired and probably won't come out again unless it's absolutely necessary."

Dad's face shows how much he misses his twin sister but I don't comment, letting him be with his memories. We head to his car with me thinking about whether I should tell him about Donovan and how I think he's involved. But I stay quiet for now.

I'M in my room on a video chat with Jack.

"I saw it on my news feed. Lucky you and the owner weren't hurt. And you think it was Donovan just by the voice?"

"And his eyes, I think he recognised me, especially

when he lunged at me. You know, I was going to try and find out if it was him and maybe tell my dad, but I'll leave that to the police, I'd better stay out of it. Constable Pathe didn't recognise me at first."

Jack laughs, "I'm sure she interviews a lot of people. But it's a good idea not to get involved, leave it to the police, they know what they're doing. Did you tell your dad about Donovan?"

"No, decided not to say anything. After he came to help out as Milly, which was just in time for me because it was only a matter of time for Hub to find me, my adrenaline rush focused on thanking dad and us being safe."

"Milly made a comeback, that's awesome."

"Yeah, she hasn't been around for ages, I think it takes a toll on my dad, he's always sad after he transforms back. He probably has vivid memories of his twin when he shapeshifts into her."

"That's understandable, she died young. And I assume being a twin, they were close."

"When he does talk about my Aunt Milly, there is definitely love there."

"Nice. On another note, have you heard from Als?"

"Yes, she and her parents were over on Saturday night. She's still on holidays from university, doesn't go back until end-Feb."

"Ha, I'm looking forward to those holiday breaks if I go to uni.

"We have less than a year to go. I'm still thinking of taking a gap year. You?"

"Maybe. It's more yes than no."

We continue the conversation for another half hour when I start yawning. "Hey, it's been a big day, see you tomorrow." I shut my laptop placing it on the floor. Sleep comes easily as I continue yawning.

IN OUR USUAL lunch spot under the Jacaranda tree, we're discussing what happened at the convenience store. We're all here – Jack, Chloe, Manuel, Aaron, Tahlia and Georgia. I filled everyone in on how it all had unfolded.

"You were lucky nothing happened to you. Transforming without any of us around was not a good idea. What if you had been hurt? That thug could have jumped you or kicked you."

"Well he didn't, did he Chloe. It was one on one and he was in shock seeing a cat, which made him slow to react. Anyway, Milly the Cat turned up in time to help. The police haven't contacted me and I have nothing to talk to them about, so leaving it all to them. And yes, I'll be more careful and make sure one of you is around next time."

"Well, as I said, that was lucky for you."

We continue talking about how my dad was driving past and stopped to help, who we think was behind the robbery, (we all suspect that gang is behind it) and how we're going to keep thinking of ways to deal with these thugs.

Jack, who has been quiet up till now, starts telling us about yet another fight he had with his brother, Matt. He's tapping his finger on his knee, I can see frustration on his drawn face. "You know I have a lot of patience but it's wearing thin with him. He seems to have no respect for my stuff or my privacy and walks around the house oblivious to anyone else being there. Our parents have had enough too. But nothing seems to bother him, no matter how often they talk to him about being more considerate."

"What was the fight about this time?"

"Taking and using my stuff again, Logan. He took my white Nike sneakers without permission and I found them under his bed - mud soaked and beginning to mould. Did I lose it!"

"I don't blame you. If I had a brother who did that, I'd lose it too. What a dropkick."

"My brother is trouble and if he keeps going down this path, he's going to get into trouble. Big trouble!"

I feel bad for Jack, but not having a sibling I really have nothing to contribute. We keep talking until the bell goes on our first day of school of the last year for Jack, Manuel, Aaron and me.

AFTER SCHOOL, we four boys are walking home. We take the short cut through the park and are sitting at the table where we have our geek group meetings when Donovan and Parker appear from behind the trees. They have grown into themselves since I last saw them, Donovan has filled into his lanky body with his beady eyes still small yet menacing. Parker, no taller than last year, but he has bulked up, his stocky body is now muscular. Of the two, Parker gives out scarier vibes, his look is more threatening. And even more so that he remains quiet.

"You, Logan ..." Donovan addresses me with disdain, "what did your weirdo father do to us? He is one of those magical people we all hear the rumours about. You know what people think about magic, they don't trust it."

I look at the others and whisper, "Stay calm" as I address my two least liked people in the world. "Don't know what you're on about, Donovan. We're just minding our own business and going home, so ..."

"You're full of it, aren't ya? Ok, so you don't want to talk about your father and his so-called powers, but there has always been somethin' fishy 'bout your family. We're keeping an eye on all of you. Your family too, Jacky.

"Nothing to keep an eye on. We're just normal members of the Glenndale community. Not like you thugs causing trouble all the time." I reply trying to look as menacing as possible, which I'm sure I'm failing at.

"None of ya business what we do and we have our gang protecting all of us. But take this as a warning, if you're ever in our way again, especially with that magic shit, you will get hurt. So, mind ya own business, right." With this he and Parker turn and walk back behind the trees.

We all let out our breath, happy nothing more happened and head towards our homes.

When Jack and I are outside my place, Jack says, "Enjoy the weekend Logan and try not to worry about those drop-kick bullies."

"Yeah, you too, bro. I do wish they would bloody well get a life." Jack has starting walking to his place, he turns backwards and while walking, nods in agreement.

THAT NIGHT while at home having dinner, I tell my parents about the incident at the park.

"It's a worry they remember what happened and that it was me who cast the spell. I'm not as good with the memory spell, Leafia is the master of that one." Dad is talking about the goblin who heads the magical goblins, she is a formidable force in the magical society.

"I'm just glad none of you were hurt, it was only a warning this time."

"Sally, we need to do something serious to stop these bullies, especially they are now part of that gang."

I listen to them discussing how they will go to the A-Alliance house and talk to Ester, the head of the committee and Leafia as well. I know they will find a solution and fix the issue that Donovan and Parker remember they were paralysed with a spell placed on them by my father. Our magical secret is in danger of being discovered and this is a huge problem for all of us magicals.

FOUR

Edward
   Father and Son

MY DAD PARKS the car in front of the derelict house that is actually the headquarters of our magical society, the A-Alliance. When we enter, we hear voices coming from the kitchen and head that way.

"Ah, hello Edward, hi Logan. You both know Leafia?"

I greet Ester and nod towards Leafia, the Goblin. "Hello Leafia, nice to see you again." I bend and offer her my hand and she shakes it.

"Hi, Edward. And who is this strapping young man?"

"Oh, this is Logan. My son."

"Pleased to meet you Logan. Officially that is. We did meet briefly when I was here last for the vote. Isn't it grand that your dad is still on the committee. We haven't heard from the other idiots have we?" she asks Ester and me.

Leafia is referring to The Five, a group that wanted me out of the magicals committee because I am not a full magical. My powers were bestowed to me by my twin sister when she passed years ago, I wasn't born magical and this was a major sticking point for this angry group.

"No," answers Ester, "The Five group has disappeared never to be seen again. I hope. You're here to stay Edward. Now, let's sit so we can discuss why we are all here."

We make ourselves comfortable around the kitchen table, which is large enough to fit twelve around it and towering over it is the trunk of the Jacaranda tree that guards the house for us. This tree, not visible from the street, is a magical tree only we magicals can see. It has been dormant for many years, not since 1908 has it had to warn magicals of non-magicals entering the house. There have been other alerts but only when magicals have entered the front or back gate, not the house itself. The tree sent out alerts to all the committee when the three children broke into the house through a window they smashed. Three of the committee members where on the scene and foiled the children's plan to go any further than the lounge area. If they had come into the kitchen and seen the tree growing indoors or had they gone out into the meadow where all the magical animals roam free, all hell would have broken loose.

Since that event there have been more magical powers added to the shield of the tree and even though the tree stands guard all the time, it won't send out alerts through the shield again unless other non-magicals breach the gates or break into the house.

Ester asks me what has happened with the bullies since I used the paralysis magic on them. "Well, they haven't learned their lesson, even though their futures involved bloodshed and gaol time. I guess the memory spell erased some of their memory, but not enough as they didn't actually learn from what the spell was showing them. We suspect they recently targeted some convenience stores in robberies too. And in broad daylight, the idiots."

"But you're not sure it was them?"

"We're almost sure it was them. Logan happened to be in one of the stores and was asked to leave by one of the three robbers that were in the store, he thinks he recognised the voice."

"That's right, I think it was Donovan, he's now part of a gang the police are keeping a watch on. They haven't made any arrests yet, so maybe it wasn't them."

"Let's keep an eye on them too, maybe that paralysis spell needs to be tweaked to work better. We need to frighten them enough to change their lives for the better. The issue is, they awoke remembering you placed the spell on them, is that right, Edward?

"Unfortunately, yes. I did go back around four in the morning to cast the memory spell, but it obviously wore off quickly. I should have asked you to do that part, Leafia."

"Right, then we goblins will have to look at that spell too, all of us need to know how to use the memory spell affectively, it is our most used one."

Continuing along the discussion of spells and how they work, we talk for another half an hour.

"Right, thanks everyone, I think we have covered everything. Come on, let's go outside and join the others." We all stand and follow Ester.

Walking out to the meadow, we see magicals enjoying themselves on this late summer Saturday afternoon. The sun slowly dipping, the sky's hue of deepening pinks and reds giving a faint glow to the gathering. It's a pleasant temperature now, the heat of the day going the way of the sky's colour.

The reason we are gathered this time is to begin the proceedings for another year after the Christmas break. Magicals take a six-week break from Christmas Day so everyone can enjoy time with family and friends without thinking about magic and doing good deeds for the non-magicals.

Part of the charter for our magical society is to help non-magicals keep safe, this was written into the charter by the first committee members headed by Santiago Rodriguez, a doctor whose job it was to heal and protect people. We do good without showing how or why we do so, it is our gift to non-magicals. My dream is to one day stamp out bullying everywhere, not just in schools. Gangs like the one Donovan is a part of are in our sights. Their robberies by bullying people to give them their hard-earned money has to be stopped.

The education department has implemented a *No Tolerance* rule to bullying in all schools and it has been successful. I am proud of doing my part to have this rule implemented, it's the reason I, someone who inherited my magical powers from my deceased twin sister, is now part of the committee of this secret society. I was voted in, and despite a breakout group trying to force me out, I was honoured the majority of the magicals wanted me to stay on the committee.

Ester walks up to the stage and readies herself at the lectern while Logan, Leafia and I find Sally.

"I assume everything went well in there?" she whispers as Ester begins the proceedings.

I answer her, "Yes, I explained what happened with the paralysis spell working at capacity on those bullies but not the memory one. Leafia and her team are looking at tweaking both spells so they work better together."

"And Leafia is here with some news, do you know what it's all about?"

"I'm not sure, but I think we're about to find out." We all turn our attention to what Ester is saying.

"… so, unfortunately there was almost an incident where children were playing near the grounds of this house and they stumbled on the back gate. The shield protects the gate and we were alerted, the children were dealt with by committee members who came onto the scene quickly and we are grateful they did. Thank you to the three of you. This proves we need to be vigilant of non-magicals entering our space, please discourage any children who want to play in and around this house."

We all applaud as the three committee members who were on the scene quickly bow their heads in acknowledgement.

"On another note, it has come to the committee's attention the paralysis and memory spells are not working as they should, more so the memory one. We will be looking into this and alert you with any updates as they come about. Please ensure once you receive the final alert you update your skills, erasing non-magicals memories of incidents is important. Leafia and her team have ensured the non-magicals have all had the memories of recent incidents erased, for now we are safe again."

"Now, I would like to invite Leafia to the stage, she has some important news for us all. Please make her welcome." Ester moves back to allow Leafia to stand on the three steps that are moved into place so we can all see her.

"Thank you and good evening to you all. As Ester has said, we are looking forward to another year of events for the magicals and we, the goblins, will be involved in many of them. We appreciate being asked to join in after successfully helping with the vote last year, the one allowing Edward Shipley to stay on the committee." There are cheers and whoops as I acknowledge the crowd, grateful to still be a part of this society.

Leafia continues when the noise dies down, "We have discussed an event with the committee and they have agreed we should host a ball to introduce up and coming young magicals and goblins who show an aptitude to keeping our secret safe while doing good deeds." Again, the crowd erupts.

I listen on as Leafia continues to share details of this event, but my mind is on the children who come to play here, are they sent by the bullies to make trouble? I will have to investigate this and decide to discuss it with Sally first and then the committee if I need to.

We're in the car, I'm driving us home after what was a pleasant afternoon and evening at the A-Alliance house, the Magicals headquarters. Everyone was buzzing about the ball to take place in June, there was much discussion about the awards and who should be invited. Ester asked the committee to liaise with Leafia and her team of goblins to bring this event to fruition. I decide to ask both Sally and Logan what they think about the bullies being behind the children playing at the house.

"What makes you think they have anything to do with it, Dad? I think they are random kids playing about."

Sally pipes in too, "Why would the bullies be involved, do they know the house is our headquarters? I don't think they do."

"Hmm, you may be right. I'm suspicious of everything now, every incident seems to come back to the bullies and that gang, or at least that's my thinking."

"Dad, I know you were bullied mercilessly at school, but that gang is not behind every problem in Glenndale."

"Ok, I'm probably over-thinking it. But how about this ball Leafia is behind, what a great idea to promote you young ones."

Logan laughs, "A bit lame, I think. Isn't having a ball a bit old-fashioned? Now, a rave ... that would be much better."

I look towards Sally who shrugs her shoulders then says, "He has a point. I might put this to Ester, maybe the A-Alliance needs to keep up with the times."

FIVE

Logan
The Birthday Parties

EVERYONE IN ATTENDANCE at my 18th birthday knows about us Magicals. All of my friends have been told and are sworn to secrecy, which is why my parents were able to book the A-Alliance grounds for this party. Even Matt, Jack's little brother, who towers over Jack's small frame now, has been warned if he so much as whispers the secret to another non-magical, he will be in huge trouble. My dad had used the paralysis spell on him and spooked the hell out of him when he saw a future he wasn't proud of. Matt doesn't want to be an outcast, at least for now. I don't trust Matt and we all still keep an eye on him.

"This place is awesome, Logan. What a great place to have a party," says Matt, his face beaming with enthusiasm.

"It is and I think the animals like having us young ones around, we give them some attention. The adults don't bother, maybe because they're used to seeing these magical creatures."

Jack pipes in, "How can you ignore them, look how cute those Llamas are, the Unicorns, and those fairies ... I just can't ..."

Both Matt and I laugh at Jack's animated face, "You're such a kid, Jack. Come on, it's time for me to cut my cake."

I look out at my family and friends – Jackson, Trudi and their daughter, Chloe, my almost-cousin. Athena and Nigel with Ailsa, Noel and Hannah with Jack and Matt, my grandmother, Vanessa and my grandparents Bill and Elizabeth, my mother's parents. These are the people I love the most and I hope they will always be a part of my life. With everything that happens with the bullies, I rely on these people to stop any crazy thoughts. It's so easy for my mind to head towards dark places after being bullied.

My friends, Manuel and Aaron, Tahlia and Georgia, along with others from our geek crew, all of them make my life special. I clear my throat and begin my speech holding back my emotions, "Thanks all of you for coming to my 18th, I know many of you like me have had a few drinks, enjoyed the food and each other's company. This will continue, I promise, so I'll keep this short. Many thanks for your gifts, I look forward to opening them later. Now, let's crank up the music and keep enjoying ourselves." Cheers swell from everyone, which are only silenced by the music starting to pump.

Dad walks up to me and slaps me on the shoulder, "Well done, Logan." He indicates for the music to be turned down temporarily. "I'd like to add a few words on behalf of your mother and I ..." He turns towards me, "Logan, you are a man now and we have watched you grow into a respectable young man with many friends." He stops and lets the mild clapping and cheers die down, "We're very proud of you, Happy Birthday, son." He grabs me in a hug and again, I struggle to keep my emotions in check. I'm lucky to have family and close friends I can trust.

Shaking with emotion I take deep breaths and head to where the others are dancing and join in. Nothing like some daggy dancing to scare away any unwanted thoughts.

MY BIRTHDAY CELEBRATIONS continue the following weekend at our local, The Glenndale Arms, with everyone from my school year plus all the geeks who don't know about our secret society, the ones I couldn't invite to the A-Alliance house, joining in.

Ailsa is by my side, "How lucky are you having two celebrations. Happy birthday." She holds up her spritzer and I clink it with my beer.

"Thanks Als, I appreciate you coming to both."

"Yeah, well, just the one drink I'm afraid. I have a uni friend who's celebrating a birthday today, so will be leaving soon." She gives me a sad face to which I laugh.

"Oh, look at you faking at being so sad to be leaving ..."

"Of course." She joins me in laughing, "you know I wouldn't want to leave my best mate's party, but my other friends ..."

"Ok, ok, I get it. You have other friends besides Jack, Chloe and me."

"But we'll always be the Awesome Foursome." She giggles at the group name our parents' bestowed on us when we were young. I had forgotten about it, "Ha, yes we will."

With all of us combined, we have taken over the back section of the pub and I'm being backslapped, congratulated, given drinks, and my face hurts from kisses the girls have given me. Not that I'm complaining about that. Being eighteen doesn't suck at all and I'm so ready to keep this party going.

Later in the evening, Jack, Chloe and I are walking out of the pub, the last ones left at my party. We're heading to the Uber waiting for us when Donovan, Parker, Cole and Maddox come out from the pub's side entrance.

"Lookee who had another birthday." Donovan slurs his words, the others look like they've had more than a few too.

I whisper to Jack and Chloe to ignore them and open the car door saying, "Get in."

"Well, how bloody rude! Not even a hello, hey Logan?"

"Logan, get in the car," urges Jack after he and Chloe had moved over in the back seat.

Before I can, the driver takes off with Jack slamming the door to avoid hitting a parked car. The driver doesn't get far because just as he passes where the bullies are standing, there is an almighty screech as he stops and Jack and Chloe jump out of the car. The driver speeds off, so much for him helping us out.

The bullies are standing ominously quiet while staring towards me. Donovan asks me what is in the bag I'm holding. They are a few presents my friends had given me. "Nothing that interests you," I blurt back at him as Jack and Chloe join me.

"Listen Donovan, we haven't seen you in a while and it's been peaceful, so let's keep it that way," implores Jack.

The four bullies are now close to us, close enough for us to smell the booze on them. They are startled for a minute as a few other stragglers fall out of the pub's front door. Donovan waits until they're out of sight then says, "Aww, Jacky, you didn't miss us, hey? Well, we missed you guys.

Now, Logan, how about giving us that bag, we'll take it off your hands."

"Like I said Donovan, there's nothing in here that interests you."

"I'll decide that, now hand it over. Or maybe you prefer I rearrange your face?"

I stifle a laugh as I see how cocky Donovan is with the three others backing him up. It's a nervous laugh because I am worried what they have in mind for us. I decide the presents are not worth us getting into a fight for, so I put the bag on the ground, "Here, knock yourself out." Then I turn to Jack and Chloe yelling, "Run." They burst into action following me to a side lane where we all transform and linger behind the garbage bins as the bullies, who were only a few minutes behind, follow us into the laneway.

"Where the fu ..." Donovan looks around wondering where we've gone, this lane is a dead end. "How the hell did they disappear? And they say they're not using magic." I can see the others begin to look for us so we scoot under the bins. It's damp and there is a putrid rotting smell.

The bullies open the largest of the bins and complain profusely about the smell. I hear Donovan say that if we've hidden ourselves in there, then we can stay there. Then he latches the bin. It's locked.

A few minutes later, we see them walk away muttering what a waste of time this was. We crawl out from under the bins and wait, making sure they are long gone. We transform back and head back to where we were standing before. To my surprise, the bag of presents is still on the ground.

Now all we want to do is get home and into our showers because the smell from that garbage has made us smell rank.

SIX

Tahlia
Waiting for Logan

MILLER AND SCARLETT walk up to us at our spot near the Jacaranda tree and I flinch a little, I don't trust them and neither does Georgia. The boys, Logan and Jack, Manuel and Aaron are on a sports retreat so we're sitting on our own.

"Hi ladies," smiles Miller, "mind if we sit?"

We don't answer and she and Scarlett sit anyway. "Hope we aren't interrupting anything, we wanted to sit here because it's cooler. Hot again today, eh?"

"Hmm." This is all I want to say but my curiosity is piqued. "Did you two want something?"

Miller looks aghast, "Why would you ask that? No, just want a cool spot, that's all. Hey, it's quiet without the boys here?"

Georgia looks at me and whispers, "Just ignore them."

So we continue our conversation about a show we've both been watching.

"Like I said, it's quiet without the boys. You know, we should hang out more, even when the boys are back. This being mine and Scarlett's last year at school, we should get to know each other better."

I can't believe what I'm hearing and look towards Georgia who I'm sure is thinking the same thing. These two have bullied us throughout our high school years and now they want to be friends. Are they serious?

When we don't answer, Miller continues, "We should keep in touch when we finish, too. Like real friends do."

I can't keep my thoughts quiet any longer, "Are you for real, Miller? And Scarlett, you're in on this too? Why would we want to be friends with you two after all the shit you have put us through, you and your degenerate boyfriends."

"Donovan and Parker aren't our boyfriends anymore, we both broke it off with them when they joined that stupid gang. That idiot, Cole, I can't stand him."

Well this is a total surprise but I'm not sure I believe them. "Really? You finally realised what dropkicks they are."

"Yeah we did. We're better off without them. Anyone special in your lives?"

I'm about to answer Miller that it's none of their business but before I can, the bell chimes and we need to head back to class. I was glad of that because I wasn't that interested in continuing the conversation.

AFTER SCHOOL, Georgia and I meet Ailsa at the shopping centre. I tell her about what happened at lunchtime.

"You're kidding. Miller and Scarlett want to be your friends. Really?" She drags out the word really.

"I'm not kidding. And they're not seeing Donovan and Parker, they broke their relationships off. Apparently, Miller hates the leader of the gang they've joined. I think his name is Cole."

"Hmm, that sounds suss. They're probably lying to get in with you two. And why would you two want to be friends after what those bullies have done to all of us over the years?"

"That's exactly what I said." Georgia replies after taking a gulp of her milkshake. The three of us are sitting at a café in the shopping centre. "I don't want anything to do with them, Als. I think they only want to be friends so they can spy on us and the boys, then tell Donovan and the rest of them where we go and what we do."

"Ha, that sounds about right. I'd stay away from them if I were you."

"I hear you both, but I was a bit curious to see what would happen if we let them in for a bit, they may have changed since breaking up with those idiots."

"Not likely, Tahlia," says Georgia. "Once a bully, always a bully."

Ailsa nods in agreement, "I agree with Georgia. Tahlia, you're delusional. Don't get involved with them. Now, I have news." Her face lights up, "I'm seeing someone."

Before we can answer, a waiter asks if we want anything else as the café is closing soon. I look at both of them and we all say no. With this, we finish our drinks and decide to browse the shops while we talk.

"That's awesome news, Als. Come on, spill."

"He's a uni student like me, Tahlia, he's studying criminal law and is a year ahead of me. His name is Kendric."

She fiddles with her phone and shows us a photo of the two of them.

We see a photo of Als with a dark-haired man, with eyes a brooding deep grey, who is slightly taller than Ailsa's petite frame. They make a good-looking, petite couple. *Can a man be described as petite?*

"He was born in Texas but his parent's moved here when he was ten. He has a slight southern accent that I find so sexy." She giggles and waves her hand in front of her face feigning cooling herself. "So hot."

"Aww, happy for you Als. Can't wait to meet him."

"Soon, Tahlia. I was going to bring him to Logan's birthday but we were just friends at the time. He only asked me out after the party. I'll organise a dinner with everyone so you can all meet him."

"Wow, so soon? Are you sure, Als?"

"Georgia, he and I have known each other for two years, so yes, I'm sure. Besides, I don't want to wait forever like Tahlia is. Has Logan asked you out yet?"

I let out a sigh, "No, not yet." We're standing outside a fashion shop and decide to sit, there are bench seats in the middle of this level. We had been talking too much to do any browsing anyway. "I'm not sure he feels that way about me."

"You've got that wrong, he talks about you all the time when I've been with him. Believe me, he notices you."

"Then what the hell is taking him so long? I've given him hints, I haven't made it a secret that I like him."

"Ok, it sounds like a job for me to move this along. Leave it with me."

I nod, but I don't know whether to laugh or cry, Als is known to stuff things up sometimes with her mothering ways.

. . .

AILSA KEEPS her promise and we're all at dinner with her and Kendric at our local Chinese. Logan and Jack, Chloe, Georgia with a guy she's dating – Blake, I think his name is. Georgia has a habit of dating only for the short term. Manuel and Aaron are coming too, they'll be here soon.

Kendric is telling us about the little he remembers of Texas, they lived in a small country town on acreage. He had his own horse and still rides when he can. "The weather was similar to Sydney back then, hot and dry in summer and not much cooler in winter. With global warming who knows what's happening now. But enough about me, tell me more about yourselves."

We each tell him our stories, the food arrives and we have a great night together. Kendric seems like a good person, Als could do worse. Although she was quieter than usually tonight. Maybe she held back letting us get to know Kendric better. She was right about his accent, that southern drawl is sexy.

LOGAN DROPS me home after dinner and we briefly talk about Kendric. "He seems ok, I'm happy for Als. She was quiet, though."

"Yeah, I agree, Tahlia. But as long as Als is happy, we shouldn't judge. Want me to walk you to the door?"

"Aww, that's sweet, but no, I can manage. Didn't drink that much, you know."

"I know, just wanted to spend a bit more time with you, that's all." With that I kiss him passionately and we do spend more time together ... making out in his car.

When I do finally walk into my home, I lean back on the front door and smile, Logan and I make a good team. And I'm dating a magical, how cool is that.

The problem is … this is all in my head, what Logan had really said was, "Bye, see you 'round." And now I find myself leaning on my front door fantasising about him and me.

SEVEN

Jack
  Matt Goes Too Far

I WALK into my room to see Matt on my bed with some of my newest and best t-shirts in front of him. He is startled when I walk in, the shock on his face is visible for a second, then he's back to his bored, non-caring face. And he's been running, his B.O. is foul. "What the hell are you doing in my room and with my stuff? How many times have you been told to leave my stuff alone or ask before you take it? And you could have showered first."

"Chill will you, I'll shower when I decide. Just want to borrow a good t-shirt, I have a date and I want to impress her."

"Jesus, it's not like you don't have any of your own. Get out, go wear your own bloody clothes."

"Come on Jack, how about this Levi's one. You haven't even worn it yet, the tag is still on it."

He dangles it in front of me and I snatch it, "Get your

sweaty hands of it, I haven't decided whether I'm keeping this one."

Matt climbs off my bed, "You're an arsehole, you know that. Just want to borrow it, not keep it."

"Matt, you don't need my clothes. Now get out so I can fumigate my room."

He heads out the door and turns, "You suck as an older brother. Wish you weren't born."

With this I see red and pounce on him despite him being bigger and fitter than me. I'm punching him with an anger that's burning through my body, my whole body shakes with force. How dare he say that!

He manages to crawl away from me when I stop punching him. "You coward, wait until I tell mum and dad, you will be grounded for life."

Matt crawls the rest of the way to his room then gives me the finger as he eases himself up the door jamb. I must have hurt him more than I thought.

WE'RE at the kitchen table, our parents having given Matt his punishment – a week without his phone and he is to do all of my chores as well as his own for the week. Matt sits with his right hand under his chin, playing with what remains of his food. Mum and dad are discussing their day and me, well, I'm still angry with my bonehead brother.

He's nearly sixteen, when the hell is he going to grow up? When I look back at when we were younger, Matt has always been the troublemaker. He had a knack of making trouble for himself. And what infuriates me the most is, he doesn't think he's doing anything wrong. According to him, he does as he pleases because this is what his mind tells him. "I don't think about it twice, it's just the way I am," he had pleaded with our parents when they had punished him for this last offence of invading my privacy.

The frustration my parents felt was obvious, they didn't have any answers either. What do you say to someone who *is just the way they are?*

Matt makes a move to leave the table when Dad says, "Where do you think you're going? Clearing the table is one of the jobs you have to do this week. As well as fill the dishwasher. You can wait until we're finished."

Matt scowls at the three of us but remains quiet. For once he's acting smart.

I'm the first to leave the table and head to my room where I sit at my desk and bring up a video chat with Logan. I need to diffuse this fire of anger in my gut.

"Hi, give me a minute, finishing off this assignment."

I wait as Logan goes off screen.

"Ok done."

"I'm pissed off with Matt, he did it again. I found him in my room reeking of sweat wanting one of my t-shirts. He was sitting on my bed looking at three of them. Apparently, he had a date he wanted to impress."

"Again. When will he learn? Doesn't he have clothes of his own?" Logan laughs, "he has a date? Who would go out with Matt?"

"I'm wondering that too, maybe it's a girl from another school who doesn't know him." I clear my throat, the anger beginning to subside. "Ha, of course he has his own clothes. If anything, he has more than me. I don't get why he needs my stuff and why go into my room when he knows he's not allowed. And, get this, when my parents reprimanded him by taking his phone from him for a week, he said, *I don't think about it twice, it's just the way I am.* What the hell does that mean? He has a right to take my stuff, to enter my room?"

"That is bloody frustrating. Maybe you need to lock your room?"

"I will from now on. And the other thing, he is so wrapped up in his own little world, he doesn't answer when we speak to him. Only yesterday Dad asked him how his running and training is going and had to ask him twice. *Hey mate, I'm talking to you.* I could hear the yelling from my room with my door closed."

We continue talking about my idiot brother for a bit then change the subject to school and how Year 12 is shaping up for us. This is my final year and I need to concentrate without having Matt's stupidity derail me.

APRIL SCHOOL HOLIDAYS are nearly here and I'm looking forward to taking short breaks from studying. Sitting having lunch with Tahlia and Georgia, they are telling me about Miller and Scarlett's constant attempts at being friends. "We know they're up to something and we're ignoring them," says Tahlia.

"Yeah, they even want to hang out in the holidays," continues Georgia, "As if we're going to do that."

I know this is suspicious behaviour from the girlfriends of two of our hated bullies and add, "Of course, they want to find out what we're doing and where we are so their douchebag boyfriends can target us more."

"Exactly. And we've told them that, but they said they have broken up with Donovan and Parker. Miller told us she hates Cole. You know him, the leader of that gang."

"Yes, I know of him Tahlia, but I bet this is bullshit. Stay away from them, that's the best thing to do."

"We will ..." answers Tahlia.

Logan has just arrived and she stops talking about the bullies and looks towards Logan. "So, any plans for the holidays?" I'm noticing how she is looking at him, somewhat lovestruck.

"Nah, not really. Studying and more studying I guess."

"What, not taking any breaks? You're not joining us if we go to a movie or something?"

Logan looks like he's not too interested but says, "Well, yeah. Just depends when. Haven't really thought about the holidays, let's get through this last week first. Hey, Jack, how's things with Matt?"

I explain to the girls what Matt had done and his subsequent punishment then answer Logan, "He's as surly as shit and I'm avoiding him. And, he hasn't been around much, he goes out most nights, maybe with that girl he was trying to impress with my clothes. There is a lot less tension at home without him around. Can't say I miss his company."

Both girls shake their heads and we keep talking about my idiot brother until the bell goes. I walk into class thinking my life is better when he isn't around.

EIGHT

Edward
The Ball is Kicked Out

SALLY HAD SPOKEN to both Ester and Leafia telling them of the young people's dislike of the event being called a 'Ball'. So the Ball is now a 'Young Achievers Awards Night'. A group of young ones had renamed the event and was subsequently given responsibility for the music, the food and choosing the trophies. Sally had been pleased with this result, it gave the young magicals a sense of purpose and they can put their stamp on this event.

The committee along with Leafia and her team decided on four awards –

'Encouragement Award for most improved in Magical Studies'

Awarded to a young magical who struggled with magical spells and has improved.

'Best Deed of the Year Award'

Awarded a young magical who has helped a non-magical, possibly more than once.

'Young Achiever Award for Excellence'

For a young magical who shows intelligence and initiative as a magical and part of the wider community.

'Young Achiever of the Year Award'

For an all-rounder who assists the magical community as well as the non-magicals.

I'M SITTING with Ester and the others discussing what is yet to be done. "So, with the awards sorted, now we need to concentrate on keeping an eye of what the young ones are doing. Who is excelling, who needs the most encouragement ..."

Ester chimes in when I take a breath, "That won't be too hard and we can ask adults to give us their nominations. I have already been given some names, many are very excited about this event."

"Ok, that's good to hear. Could we wrap this up, is there anything else to discuss?" I ask this wanting this meeting over as quick as possible. I've had a tough week at work and am exhausted, I'm stifling yawns in between speaking.

There is back and forth discussion about who is doing what and minor details are tidied up. Leafia tells us how and when her team is available, their help will give this event a nice touch, goblins are creative and sensitive to young people's needs.

We finish the meeting and I head home, it's a Wednesday night and I'm happy this meeting didn't go late into the night.

. . .

ARRIVING HOME I find Sally and Logan in the lounge room having a deep discussion. Sally is sitting in the armchair, her favourite spot because this chair is an heirloom from her grandmother. I'm not a fan of it, the mainly green floral design doesn't appeal to me. Not that I would ever tell Sally that. Logan is spreadeagled on the three-seater, a more contemporary brown velvet that is *oh so comfortable* to lie on.

"Oh, hi." Sally welcomes me as I bend down to give her a light kiss. "We're discussing Matt and his latest antics."

"Yeah, the idiot has been in Jack's room again. They had a huge fight, Matt was without his phone for a week and had to do extra chores, and now you won't believe what he's done."

When Logan pauses for longer than I expect, I say, "Well, are you going to keep me in suspense? Come on, I'm beat and need to crash asap."

"Geez, Dad, chill," he says scoffing me. "He's joined the gang, the one that Donovan and Parker are a part of. By the way, the police have still not found the culprits of those convenience store robberies, but I bet you this gang has something to do with them."

I make myself comfortable on the other mismatched armchair. "Tired, that's all. And you're probably right. But why the hell has Matt joined the gang? And isn't he too young?"

"I don't think age enters into who becomes a member, Dad. Anyway, the reason he's joined is he is super pissed at his family, especially Jack. He told Jack he wishes Jack was never born. This is when Jack hit him senseless. A few days later Matt started going out at night, almost every night. At first they thought he was going out with a girl, but when

Jack's dad asked him where he was going he spat out, *'None of your damn business'*."

"Whoa, I can imagine Buster, err, I mean Noel didn't take that too well?" Every now and then I refer to Noel by the name we called him at school. The name Buster brings back too many bad memories for me. Noel is a much-reformed person now, a good dad and husband. I'm proud to call him my friend.

"He remained calm on the night, but the next night he and Jack followed Matt to the gang's headquarters. This is when Jack's dad went in and pulled him out by the collar threatening the gang members with the police if they come near Matt again. Matt is now not allowed out at night and Jack has been asked to look out for him during the day."

I rub my face with my hands and sigh, "That boy is trouble, I feel for Noel and Hannah. Hannah especially, she is a caring person and this must be awful for her. It seems Matt has taken after Noel's old bullying ways but in an even worse way." I look towards Logan who had exclaimed ...

"What the F ..." He holds himself back, his hand to his mouth. "There's been another robbery, this time at night in the shopping centre, the convenience store near the carpark."

"They've attacked another convenience store?"

"Whose they? The Gang?"

"Probably, Sally. I wouldn't put it past them."

Logan yawns, "I'd say it was them. And we need to keep an eye on Matt, he can't be trusted. I'm sure he fed the gang a lot of information on us, they have been uncannily present wherever we have been. He's probably involved in this robbery." He stretches, "Hey, I'm knackered too, see you both in the morning."

I watch as Logan staggers his lanky frame towards the

stairs. He's a good kid but so is Jack, he doesn't deserve a brother like Matt. And if Matt has been giving the gang information, this makes him even more stupid. Why does he want his brother and friends bullied?

I look over at Sally rubbing her neck, her sunken eyes show she's worried. "There must be an underlying cause why Matt keeps acting up. Is he jealous of Jack?"

"He probably is, Jack is more accomplished than him, has more friends and is more personable. That's a lot to be jealous of."

Sally stands up and moves to where I am, touching my knee lightly. "Come on, let's go to bed." She yawns as I follow her up the stairs, "I might reach out to Hannah tomorrow and see how she's coping." As we enter our bedroom, I decide I will seek out Noel too, he might want to talk about his wayward son.

IT'S our monthly games night and we're hosting at our place. Jackson and Trudi arrived a little late when I had already started a card game with Anthea, Nigel, Hannah and Noel. We have set up on our dining room table as usual.

"Sorry guys, I was on a work call and then Ailsa rang. We're here now, what are we playing?" Jackson says handing me a six pack of beer.

"Thanks," I say taking the beer and heading to the fridge, "We can start something else if you like, we were just filling in time."

Sally chimes in, "Everything ok with Ailsa?"

"Oh yes," answers Trudi, "she was telling us about her recent trip to Tasmania with her university group. You know she is finishing at the end of this year, then she's thinking about doing her master's in social work. This was a friend's trip, nothing to do with her uni work."

"Good for her, that's great. She will make a great social worker with her caring personality."

This makes me think about Hannah and look over towards her. Stress shows on her face and Noel's as well. I try to steer the topic away from our kids as I'm sure they don't want to talk about this, "So, what are we playing?"

Hannah stands up. With her eyes down, she sighs deeply saying, "Sorry guys, I have a headache coming on. Noel, let's go."

"What? We haven't even started. I'm sure Sally can give you some painkillers."

"I need to lie down, I'm feeling nauseous. Sorry everyone."

"No need to apologise," I say.

Sally stands up saying, "I'll see you both out. Do you want some painkillers, I do have some?"

"I'm ok, thanks Sally. We have a short drive home."

Looking at Noel's face, I know he doesn't want to leave. But Hannah obviously didn't want to stay if the discussion about our kids was going to continue or came up again later.

I'M in my office at work and decide to call Noel. He answers at the first ring.

"Hi Edward, sorry about Saturday night. Hannah was … well, she wasn't feeling great."

"No need to apologise, is she feeling better?"

"It's Matt, she is worried about him and it manifests in her stomach doing backflips and random headaches. Our son is giving us hell."

"Logan filled us in on what happened, sorry he's such a handful."

"When I found out he was part of that gang, that was the final straw. We had to do something drastic. But now, he's grumpy and unreasonable at home making our life miserable. He doesn't talk to us, acknowledge us ... I'm so over him."

"Well, just letting you know Sally and I are here for you. Call us anytime, both of you."

"Thanks Edward, I appreciate that." He clicks off the call with a despondence I've never heard in Noel's voice.

NINE

Sally
Reaches Out

I'M SITTING at the café outside the shopping centre waiting for Hannah. The table I chose is near the window inside, it's chilly out. The weak sunshine gives this spot a little warmth.

As I wait I look out at our quaint suburb with the leaves on trees beginning to colour in oranges and browns, some losing their leaves already and they crunch under peoples' feet. As Sydney suburbs go, Glenndale is a middle-class one with many growing families. I watch as people go about their business on this cloudy autumn day.

Hannah sits down apologising she's late. She isn't, I was early but I don't say anything until she's comfortable. "I'm glad you came, you were hesitant when I called you."

"No, umm yes, a little. I know what you want to talk about."

"We don't have to talk about Matt if you don't want to. You told me some things when we spoke the other day."

"It's crazy, Sally. He is all I think about. I worry whether his temperament is going to get him in real trouble. He's irresponsible and doesn't seem to care."

I take this as a sign that Hannah does want to talk about her youngest son. I had taken the liberty to order coffee for me and a tea for Hannah, which is served before I begin. "I'm listening if this is what you want to talk about."

She drops her eyes then looks up for me to see her green eyes glistening with tears. She sniffs, "I think I need to talk about it because I'm driving myself nuts. Jack is the one who has been a breeze to parent, Matt ... well, you know. And Noel, I have to keep him calm because who knows what he will do to Matt, his anger can be unbridled."

I'm remembering some of the stories Edward had told me about Noel during his bullying days as I wait for Hannah to compose herself. "I'm doing my best to keep Matt calm while Jack keeps his father busy. Since the gang thing with Noel dragging him out so embarrassingly, I don't think Matt has been near any of those thugs. This is a blessing and maybe he has learned his lesson. He and Jack are basically ignoring each other." She blows her nose and sips her tea.

Not really sure what to say, I wait in case she wants to say anything else. When she doesn't, I say, "Hannah, both Edward and I are here to help. I know Edward has spoken to Noel. I'm at a loss of what else to say. Maybe Matt has turned a corner now."

"Maybe. I don't want to see him going down that path of destruction with those gang members, my heart breaks when I think what trouble he could have found himself in if we hadn't found out what he was up to. From what I hear from Jack, that gang is not to be messed with."

"Logan seems to think they are the ones involved in those robberies, the convenience store ones. The police haven't made any arrests yet."

"Jack thinks that too but I asked him to stay out of it, leave it to the police. He was threatening to go with Logan to the headquarters, where they would hide and transform so they could listen in on them. Then this happened with Matt and he's forgotten about that, I hope."

I try to remember if Logan mentioned anything about that but can't recall. Hannah's face is drawn so I change the subject to books and what I've read lately, this is an easier subject to deal with. I see her visibly relax to be talking about something else.

Later that day, I'm home discussing the Matt situation with Logan. Sitting at the kitchen table, he's devouring some blueberry muffins I baked. I had only taken them out of the oven a few minutes before, how he's not burning his mouth is beyond me.

"Hannah looks terrible, this is really messing with her. She is worried Matt might seek out the gang again. Which reminds me, were you and Jack planning on visiting their headquarters?"

"Umm, not really," he says swallowing hard. He'd put almost a whole muffin in his mouth. "I brought up the subject to Jack but we weren't serious about it. Remember I told you about the thug in the convenience store who told me to beat it sounded like Donovan?" I nod yes. "Well, for a minute I wanted to find out. Then Jack and I threw some other ideas around but between our studying and Matt, we forgot about it."

Relief seeps through me, "You don't know how glad I

am to hear that. Smart choice. Now, the other thing I wanted to discuss is the Awards night, we're going to need your help with distributing flyers and contacting your magical friends overseas."

"I can do that, will organise a team with my friends. Thanks Mum, the muffins were sick," he says standing, picking up his backpack and heading up to study.

I'm smiling as I watch him walk up the stairs, he's our only son and I'm thankful he's responsible, unlike Matt. I tidy up the kitchen and take out my laptop to finish some work emails while I wait for Edward to come home, I'm sure we'll be discussing Matt again tonight.

Edward and I are sitting in our lounge. Logan is upstairs studying.

"Ok, the awards ceremony is all set." He continues telling me what has been discussed at the latest committee meeting and the kids who have been nominated. It's an impressive list of young magicals, something we adults should be proud of.

When he finishes what he has to say, I ask, "Have you spoken to either Noel or Hannah this week?"

"Noel has called me about work stuff and I did ask how things were with Matt. Not much has changed, he's still being an arse, but at least he isn't going to the gang head-quarters."

"That's a relief. Hopefully he's not keeping in touch with them via text."

"Well, yes, he could be. Who knows what crap they are filling his brain with, especially about Jack. That gang seem to target Jack and Logan more than others and I'm proud of how they handle themselves, both are well-adjusted kids considering what has been thrown at them."

I nod in agreement, pleased Logan has a good friend like

Jack, they look out for each other. Standing up I offer Edward a cup of tea, which he turns down for a scotch instead. As he heads to get that, I go to make tea for me.

With the jug boiling, I think about Hannah, she isn't handling the situation with Matt too well and I'm glad to be there for her when she needs me. For someone as caring as Hannah, Matt has become too much to handle.

TEN

Edward
Young Achievers Awards Night

WE COMMITTEE MEMBERS along with Leafia and her team are all dressed in our ceremonial robes. These are not used often and mine needed airing for weeks as I'm sure was the case for everyone else's too. In years gone by, the robes were used more often but times have changed. Logan was right not wanting this night referred to as a ball, it was taking us back into the past. Showing young people how proud we are of them and their achievements is a good thing, but it has to be relatable to them.

I pull my robe around me, at least it is keeping me warm on this cool wintry night.

I can see Logan with Jack and Chloe sitting at our table. Sally is standing up talking to Hannah and Noel. I'm glad they are able to make it tonight, things with Matt seem to have settled down, he has behaved himself since the gang incident. I see Jackson and Trudi walk up to them. Even though they are not magicals, they have been invited because their daughter Chloe has been nominated for an award.

I also take in the whole scene, there are over five hundred of us magicals, gathered from all over the world. We have decorated the meadow with lights, flowers and plants. Fairy lights adorn the plants. There are also portable heaters set randomly, although everyone is rugged up.

The formalities begin after everyone has sampled the starters, Ester welcoming everyone. "Thank you all for attending our inaugural 'Young Achievers Awards Night',

where we are showcasing our young people and their efforts during the past year. I am proud of all the nominees, you are all winners in my eyes. So, let's give a big hand for all of our young people." Once there is quiet again, Ester continues explaining what the awards are about and how they are meant to encourage young magicals to do their best. "Now, please enjoy your meal. Leafia and I will be back to continue the ceremony later."

"Dad, do you think this will end on time? We want to meet Als and other friends after this."

"As long as the award winners keep their speeches short, I'm sure it will end by eleven."

"I'll take that as a yes because I know others who want to go out when this is done."

I smile and turn towards Sally who is speaking with Hannah and Noel. Thankfully, not about Matt. Trudi and Jackson are also sitting with us.

"Thanks for inviting us, Edward. What a spread we have here."

"With Chloe nominated of course we had to invite you two. You're our special guests who we trust will keep our secret."

"I made that pact with you long ago, remember? Back in high school during our early years when you told me about this amazing society."

"I remember. You were the first non-magical I told, Trudi. There are quite a few of you now, all helping us to keep our secret."

"There have been times when I've been tempted to sell the story to the media ..."

"What, you wouldn't?" I can't believe what I am hearing.

"Relax, Edward, I'm joking. As if I would do that after all we've been through ... although the money would have come in handy," Trudi laughs.

I have to agree she is right but am glad to hear she was only joking. There have been many instances where our secret could have been exposed, we're lucky to have the memory spell putting an end to any problems.

We continue chatting and reminiscing about our school days, which feel like they weren't that long ago. Now we all have children, our lives are full of drama occasionally but mainly, we're all content.

When it's time for the awards, we have finished dessert and with champagne in hand we listen to Ester and Leafia.

They each read out names of the nominees for the first award – the Encouragement Award for most improved in Magical Studies

"And the winner is – Sofia ..."

We can't even hear her last name over the cheers and clapping. A young girl who I know is thirteen but looks younger, walks up to Leafia and accepts her award. She declines to say a speech as she is too shy. I'm sure Logan and his young friends will be happy about that.

Next is the Best Deed of the Year Award

"And the winner is – Carlos Deljavo, who helped an elderly couple with daily tasks over this past year without expecting anything in return. Give Carlos a big hand." Leafia didn't have to say this as his large family had already erupted into congratulatory cheers.

Our Young Achiever Award for Excellence goes to – Travis Campbell.

"Hey, isn't that the kid I met at my first visit here, Mum? Remember he had a voice he could change into an opera singer."

"Yes, that's him, Logan. He has an incredible skill with accents and singing voices. He also has other powers that he has put to good use."

"Good for him, I'll congratulate him on my way out. Now comes the exciting one, I'm sure this is yours, Chloe."

I see Chloe's face turn a rosy, red as Logan takes her hand and then turns to concentrate on what Leafia is saying.

"And now for our Young Achiever of the Year Award ..." She takes her time for affect. "Chloe Walker." Chloe has been active in the community helping other young magicals with studies and ...

The cheers coming from our table again drown out the rest of what Leafia is saying. There is even more applause and cheers as Chloe makes her way to the stage.

I am amazed at how Chloe has grown into this young woman with ambition, she definitely takes after her mother. With her auburn hair flowing to her shoulders, the green strapless dress she is wearing matches her green eyes. She takes the trophy from Leafia and shyly takes the microphone. Sniffling she thanks everyone and congratulates the other winners and nominees.

She walks back to our table to applause erupting once

again. Trudi and Jackson envelope her in hugs and kisses. We all congratulate her individually as she wipes her eyes. "Thank you all of you, this is an honour. And for just being me and doing what I love."

"You're a natural born leader, Chloe, you deserve this. Now, how about more champagne and then you Jack and I can go to meet the others. I'm sure Als will be wanting to share in your glory."

Travis comes over to congratulate Chloe too. We all give him our congratulations as well. Logan congratulates him with Travis slapping Logan on the shoulder, he obviously remembers him. "Good to see you again, Logan. You're doing great too, I've been watching your progress."

"Thanks Travis, I appreciate that. Well, we're off to have a good time, join us if you like."

"You going to The Arms?" Logan nods. "Then sure, will do."

We watch as they leave when Ester and Leafia come and sit at our table and we thank them for doing a great job at hosting this night.

"It was good, wasn't it? Those kids are so deserving, I'm sure we'll have more nominees next year," says Leafia. "But I see the young ones have disappeared already."

"Yes, they're off to meet up with friends, it is a Saturday night after all." Everyone smiles as we continue drinking and talking until late in the evening.

ELEVEN

Logan
   A Troubling Night

WE ARRIVE at The Arms and the place is packed with the usual Saturday night crowd. A few people acknowledge us as we walk through looking for our friends. It's amazing that we can hear Als' scream as she sees us even with the live music's pumping sound. "Ooh, hey, you all made it. Hi, I'm Ailsa, but call me Als," she places her hand out to Travis after greeting the three of us.

"Pleased to meet you," says Travis eyeing Als up and down. Looks like Travis might be taking a liking to our mother hen.

"Come on guys, I want you to meet someone. Follow me."

We're at the back of the pub where all the bench seating is and she introduces us to her boyfriend, Kendric. It looks like Travis has some competition.

"Hi, nice to meet you all. Ailsa has told me all about everyone. Especially you Logan, should I be wary of you?"

"Ha, no, Als is like a sister to me. I'm sure she told you that." *But you might have some competition in Travis. Tonight is going to be interesting.* Kendric is the same height as Als, although she has heels on, so Travis has height in his favour. But what do I know about what my friend likes in men.

Tahlia walks up to me and says hello as I see Als and Chloe walk towards the bar. "Hey you."

Is it my imagination or is she giving me an extra big smile? "Hi, umm I was about to get a drink, what are you drinking?"

"Thanks, a vodka cranberry."

I make my way through the crowd to the bar in time to see Als giving Chloe a high five, "Well done girlfriend. Although when I'd heard you were nominated I knew you would win."

"Right, of course you did. But thanks, it hasn't sunk in yet."

"Well we have the rest of the night to celebrate. Oh, hey Logan."

"Hey. Just getting drinks for Tahlia and I. By the way, where's Georgia?"

Als answers me, "She was here earlier but said something about having another party. A bit like you guys, two parties in one night. Now, Logan, make sure you treat Tahlia well tonight." She winks as they both walk away.

What the hell is she on about? I always treat Tahlia well, she's my friend.

I'm back with everyone and hand Tahlia her drink. I notice Kendric and Travis are deep in conversation with Als sitting between them. Kendric has his hand on Als' knee.

"So, what have you been up to this week? Haven't seen much of you."

"Oh, you know, busy studying. I've spent a lot of time in the library." As I am saying this Als is behind Tahlia making a heart shape with her fingers. Then she comes around in front of Tahlia, grabs my hand and drags me to a quieter spot.

"You have to give it a go with Tahlia."

"What the hell are you on about?"

"She's sweet on you, you dummy. Can't you see she's been flirting with you for ages."

"Flirting? I thought she was just being friendly."

"Friendly? Is twirling her hair when she talks to you *just being friendly*? She has been giving you puppy-dog eyes too. Honestly, Logan."

I stop and think for a minute. It's true, Tahlia has done those things. Ha, how stupid of me. "Right, thanks for letting me know. She is cute, I have noticed that. Oh, by the way, watch that Travis dude, he's been checking you out."

"Yes, unlike you I do notice these things. Two men interested in me, how cool," she laughs. "Now, off you go to woo Tahlia, I can handle my own situation.

I laugh as I walk back towards Tahlia feeling more elated that when we walked in. And I know Als will enjoy tonight with the attention of two men, the tart that she is. She has always been confident around men and men are drawn to her, not only because she is beautiful, but also because she is smart.

"What was that about? And what's with the smirk?" asks Tahlia when I'm back.

"Oh nothing, she was making sure I behave myself around you and I'm smiling about her being chased by two men tonight, Kendric and Travis."

"Ha, I noticed Travis leering at her when we walked in." Then she drops her eyes and when she looks back up to me, she is smiling. "Als can look after herself. Now, what if I don't want you to behave?"

My face burns red, which I'm hoping she doesn't see in this low light of the pub, as I direct her to a spot on one of the bench seats. We sit and talk. Over the years we have talked a lot, but not as much as we are tonight. She plays with her hair and this time I notice. I also notice the glint in her eye, this is something I haven't seen before. My lips are on hers before I can think twice. She moves in towards me as I taste the bitter cranberry. Why have I waited so long to do this?

There is a scream that stops us kissing. I look over to see Als trying to hold Kendric back, he's about to hit Travis.

"Hey, what's going on?" I ask pulling Als away before she gets hurt.

"This arsehole made a move on Ailsa. Even when he knows she's my girlfriend."

"Did you?" I turn to Travis and ask. I'm between the two of them pushing them apart with both arms.

"Nah, I just told her she looks nice in that dress." Travis is slurring his words, his body swaying.

"In front of her boyfriend, are you mad?" I push him away from Kendric and we go out to the spot where Als and I were earlier. "You don't compliment a girl in front of her man, you idiot." I can't believe I'm talking to Travis like this, I don't know him that well.

"Chill, dude. I'm heading out of here anyway, she's welcome to that guy, but she will regret it."

"What, why?"

"Just a feeling, that's all. In what I've seen tonight, he doesn't respect her."

"Bro, that's jealousy talking. I think it best if you do leave." He looks at me and nods twice, more because he's drunk than for any other reason. Then he leaves from the side gate, stopping to say, "I'm right, Logan. You'll see."

I head back to Tahlia and the others wondering what the hell Travis ingested tonight, he only just met Kendric, no different to the rest of us. How can he make such a judgement so quickly?

"It's ok everyone," I say seeing their worried faces when I come back in, "he's gone and meant no harm, Kendric, he was drunk."

"He's an arse, where the hell did he come from?"

"Just a random I know, you won't have to deal with him again. Come on, there's still time to party."

IT'S early morning and we're sitting outside the pub sobering up. Jack, Chloe, Als, Tahlia and me. What a night we've had. After Travis left we continued drinking and dancing with Tahlia showing me how much she was into me. She was attentive, her kisses were divine and I was feeling giddy too.

We're holding hands as we stand up ready to leave, another Uber waiting for us. Jack, Chloe and Als had just left in one.

Donovan and Parker head towards us. Donovan holding a cricket bat.

Shit! I'm alone with Tahlia, at this hour no one else is around. We head towards the car and I push Tahlia inside, "Stay there." Then I go to the driver's side and tell him to leave if things get ugly and to contact the police.

"Oh, look at you protecting your little friend, how

sweet. Now, Logan, we need to talk about your dad's stunt." He hits the side of the bat on his hand.

"Again. We've been through this, my dad was trying to show you how your actions will have consequences."

"Yeah, ok. What I want to know is your dad one of those weird, magical dudes? He didn't make me look good in front of my gang mates." He keeps hitting the bat on his hand and Parker moves a step closer to me. "Tell me the truth."

I stand my ground near the car, "And if he is magical, how does this affect you?"

"It's all the weird things that happen when we're around you and your friends. Jacky, Chloe, how it is you all disappear and animals attack us? We're not stupid you know, you're all magic, aren't you?"

It's hard for me not to laugh, this dumb thug has finally worked out we are magicals, but I have to avoid answering, he can't know our secret. This is escalating and I don't want Tahlia to see me getting hurt. I turn to the driver and ask him to leave, this altercation is not going to end well. I hear Tahlia calling out to me as the driver takes off.

"Me magical? Are you crazy? I'm a normal kid like you. Well, not like you, I'm a nice person."

"Are you accusing Parker and me of not being nice? We haven't pummelled you yet but keep insulting us and we will."

"Come on Don, you know you're here to pummel me. Why don't you just get on with it so we can all go home." The night is pitch black now save for a streetlight shedding a pale glow over us.

"Tell us the truth and you can go home."

"What the hell good would it do if you know whether my father is magical or not? Or me and my friends. Are you going to tell everyone about us? Not that I'm saying we are."

"It's a bloody good story, isn't it? Why shouldn't we all know about whatever it is you guys are up to."

Up to? We do good deeds, we're not *up to* anything. I'm angry and tired now and want this over with. He is still hitting the bat against his hand and Parker has moved closer to me. I can see his eyes are glazed over, both of them are high. I have to protect myself before they hurt me, so I transform in front of them.

"Fuc ... I told ya, he is one of those, Parks."

I lunge at Parker and scratch his arm. He screams.

"Why you ..." I see Donovan's leg coming for me and I move in time to avoid it but my ankle moves at a weird angle. I don't move far enough away from him because the cricket bat comes for my head.

I hear voices that are not Donovan's or Parker's and I don't remember anything after that.

TWELVE

Matt
> Keeps in Touch

MY FAMILY SUCKS, especially my too-good brother who can do no wrong in the eyes of our parents. Stuck in my room, I'm browsing YouTube on my laptop but not paying much attention. My phone was confiscated for a week and that long without your phone is a lifetime. Not that I missed much, the same lame stuff on socials, posted mainly by girls, not many messages missed cause I don't have lots of friends, but anyway, it's good to have it back. It buzzes and I see Donovan's message.

Hey, where you been

Home, been grounded after being dragged out of headquarters. F'ing embarrassing. 😠

And you're listen' to 'em. Come on bro, get back here.

You there now?

Yeah. Talkin' 'bout our latest heist. Lots of goodies to eat and drink. Come down.

I look at the time, it's only eight. Be there soon. 😄

Opening my door listening, I hear the three of them are in the lounge. Good, I can sneak out through the laundry. It'll take me twenty minutes to walk to the headquarters, will take a shortcut through the park.

I ARRIVE to shouts and hellos, "where you bin?", "hey, bro, good to see ya" and instantly feel at home. Who needs a shitty family like mine when you can have these guys?

Donovan slaps my shoulder as I walk up to him, "Matty-boy, you made it. See, ain't so hard to sneak out? Now, what you want? Chocolate, drink?"

"Ah, chocolate, thanks." He hands me a Kit Kat and I chow it down with pleasure. "So, when was this heist?"

"'Bout month or so. You've been out for a bit, missed all the action."

Parker, Maddox and Cole are sitting on the rickety stage, legs dangling. They're stoned and are shoving snacks down their throat.

"Hey there Matty, welcome back." Parker has a mouthful of chocolate, some spills on his t-shirt. He half-heartedly rubs it making it worse.

Cole jumps off the stage and walks towards me placing his hand on my back, "Walk with me young man, we need to talk." I look at Donovan who nods giving me a backward wave for me to go with our boss man. He takes me outside.

Happy I'm wearing a hoodie, I pull the hood over my head.

"So, we could have used your help, but I understand how hard it was for you to come back after your old man pulled you out of here."

"Yeah." That's all I manage, this guy is intimidating.

He's taller than me and I'm six feet. Bulked up, his tatts shine on his arm muscles. He doesn't feel the cold, he's wearing a leather vest that's seen better days. Is that sweat that's making his tatts shine?

"Don't worry 'bout that no more, you're welcome here whenever you want to come, you're part of this family now. We promise to look after our own and, if you give us the right info 'bout your brother and those idiot friends of his, you'll be rewarded."

With my hands in my pockets, I look up at him, "Rewarded? How?"

"Depends what you tell us, but things like cash, tech stuff, you know, useful things any kid your age needs."

Huh, I smile with pride, these guys are the best. I'll tell them everything I know, Jack and his douche friends won't know what's hit them. It's midnight before I leave, although I could have stayed all night, the feeling of being wanted was strong.

As I sneak back in through the laundry, the house is still. I creep to my room not wanting to be found out and crawl into bed. Can't take the smile off my face.

IT'S a week later where I had managed to sneak out twice more, Mum noticed I was in a better mood and told me she was happy to see me not so angry. I just smiled back and kept walking up the stairs. As I walk past Jack's room I hear him and someone else laughing. Probably one of his daggy friends over for a play date. I'm about to ignore them when I hear an accent ...

I stop and put my ear closer to his door when I hear the slight accent ... that's Manuel, I didn't know he and Jack were that friendly. There is silence then I hear a moan ...

whatever is going on in there is a chance for me to get Jack into trouble. I open the door.

"What the ..." Jack pulls back from kissing Manuel and Manuel scurries to put his shirt back on. He sits on Jack's bed staring at me.

"Cosy in here isn't it. A bit of afternoon delight you two, how nice."

"Matt, get the fu..."

"... out of your room. Yes, I know Jack. Forgot to lock your door this time eh? Too much love in the room to remember." Jack steps towards me, "Stop before this goes any further, just give me what I want and your secret is safe with me."

Jack laughs, "Mum and Dad already know, so no, you're not getting what you want."

"Who's talking about them, I mean the gang, I'm sure they'd like to know about you two having this ... this, what is it, a relationship? They will pummel both of you to the point no one will recognise you."

"You've gone to the headquarters again?"

"What? No, what makes you say that? But one text to Donovan and you two are toast." Jack makes another move towards me and I step towards him ready for another fight. Manuel holds him back.

Manuel stands and looks at me, derision all over his face, then blasts out, "You piece of shit, what makes you think your brother doesn't deserve to be loved. And look at you hiding behind those thugs, you coward. Go ahead, let the world know, we're not ashamed of our love."

I nearly puke when I see the soppy, loving face Jack gives Manuel. Sticking my finger in my mouth, I feign a vomit, "You two are disgusting ..." I don't finish the sentence because Jack throws me down on the floor. My head feels the brunt of it and I black out.

"Matt, can you hear me?" I vaguely hear the voice of my mother. Am I dead? "Matt, honey, please wake up."

My eyes slowly open and I focus on my mother's face, she's holding my head with one hand, the other stroking my face. When I have fully focused, Jack is sitting on his bed. Alone.

"Oh Matt, you're ok. It was just a knock, but you may need medical help. Does your head hurt?"

Forcing myself to sit up, I rub the back of my head. "Umm, no ... umm, maybe a bit."

"Come with me, I'll take you to emergency, we'd better check." She turns to Jack, "You stay here, Dad will be home soon."

She helps me stand but I can't believe what I've heard, "He's not being told off, you asked him nicely to stay put. Leave me the ... shit, I can't believe this family." I wobble out of Jack's room and make it to my own flopping onto my bed. I don't need this family or their help, they only see angelic Jack as their son.

Mum is at my door, "Matt ..."

"I don't want to talk, I don't want you here."

"Your head, we should get it checked. You may have concussion."

"It was just a knock. Leave me alone!" I yell with as much force as my head allows.

She stands there for a few minutes, then mutters under her breath that she is downstairs if I need her.

THIRTEEN

Logan
A Stint in Emergency

IT'S 4AM, I'm in emergency with an enormous headache and what I think is a broken leg. The paramedics gave me a green whistle to suck on when we were speeding to the hospital. That has worn off now.

Dad is sitting next to me on the phone to mum. "He's in a lot of pain ..."

I'm only half-listening as I'm trying to get the attention of a nurse walking into emergency, "Please, I need pain killers." She looks at me and nods then disappears through a door. I drop my head, which is stupid because it deepens the pain, but when I look up she's there handing me two tablets and a paper cup of water.

"It won't be too long now," she says kindly with a sweet smile.

Two hours later with the pain only slightly subsided, I'm resting on a bed with a drip in my arm, my right leg has an ice pack on it, and a doctor is explaining to my dad that I will need plaster because I have a broken ankle.

When the doctor leaves, Dad asks me again what happened. "Ok, we couldn't talk much in that full emergency room, explain to me now what happened."

After all the drugs my mind is blurred, but I do remember Leafia turning up to help me. "She was there with two other goblins and cast a spell on Donovan and Parker so they wouldn't remember seeing me transform. And to forget they were seeing three goblins too."

Dad laughs lightly, his face still shows concern, "So this was when you transformed back and called another uber to send them home?"

"Yes, I think so, because Don and Parks weren't there anymore when Leafia helped me to call the ambulance. But how did she know where I was?"

"Goblins scout the street at night making sure citizens are safe. She knew you were at The Arms, I had told her earlier. She had probably checked on you a few times, I know she keeps an eye on all you young magicals at night."

"Umm, wow, that's good for us. I'm sorry Dad, I didn't know what else to do but transform in front of them. Don kept questioning whether you are a magical and he worked out Jack, Chloe and I are too." I'm beginning to feel weary and close my eyes.

"It was only a matter of time someone worked it out, Logan. Rest now, we can discuss this later."

It's ten in the morning and mum is fussing over me. "Will you please go to work, I'm fine. I have everything I need right here." She had pulled a side table up to the lounge with my phone, laptop, snacks and a drink on it.

"Fine, I'm off then. Call me if you need anything, I'll be home by three."

"Thanks. Love you, Mum." She turns to me and blows a kiss.

It's a school day so I log onto the website and check what needs doing today. The last thing I feel like doing is schoolwork but this being my last year, I have to put in the hours. I'm as comfortable as a I can be with my right leg in plaster, a have a blanket and the heater keeping me warm, so I concentrate on what needs doing.

Later, I'm chatting online with Jack and Chloe.

Those two are arses, honestly, kicking a cat like that and then hitting you in the head with a cricket bat. Lucky it you had moved a little but not enough to avoid the bat.

Yeah, Chole and I should have waited for the two cars to arrive before we left in our Uber.

Thanks guys, but how were we to know those idiots were going to turn up? And Jack, I moved to avoid the bat but the edge still got me. If I hadn't moved I'm sure I wouldn't be here talking to you both.

Shit. Lucky you, but still, Donovan now yields a bat!

Yeah, he's becoming more physical in his bullying, probably due to him being part of that gang. He's salty as, his anger fuels him.

We continue chatting about how I'm feeling and managing with the crutches. The cast will be on for six weeks and lucky for me it's winter, the cooler weather will make it a little more comfortable.

I'm shovelling down the dinner my dad prepared, laying around all day has made me ravenous.

"Take it easy, Logan, you'll give yourself indigestion," laughs Mum. "Now, your father and I went to the police to report what happened to you and they told us a car did go to the scene but by the time they arrived everyone had gone."

I'm shocked, "The police, right. I had forgotten about

that, I asked the uber driver to call them. Imagine if they had turned up and seen the goblins." We all laugh a nervous laugh.

"Well, Leafia would have used another forgetting charm, but lucky for us there was no need. The police have the details and are putting pressure on the gang to come forward, specifically Donovan and Parker. They were the only ones there, right?" I nod yes to Dad and he continues, "With both you and Jack being seriously injured by those two, it's time they were taught a lesson. If that bat had hit you square on your head it would have been a king hit."

He isn't telling me anything I don't know and I sure am glad to be sitting here at our dinner table, things could have been so much worse. "Even though a Maine Coon is a larger cat, it is still small enough to dodge quickly, but I already had an injured ankle by then so wasn't fast enough."

"Well, you're lucky you only have a broken ankle and those headaches didn't persist. The police want you to go down and give a statement when you're up to it, we need to give them as much evidence to give those two a scare."

"Do you think they'll be locked up again?"

"We'd like to see that happen, but they will probably only be given a warning. Let's just hope no one is seriously injured again, or worse, dies at the hands of that gang."

"What an awful thought. Come on Logan, let me help you upstairs." I place my arm on mum's shoulder and with dad helping too, we make it to my bedroom safely.

FOURTEEN

Tahlia
Miller and Scarlett Be Gone

ANOTHER SATURDAY NIGHT OUT. Logan and I have been dating for three weeks now and I am so glad he finally realised how much I'm into him. Boys can be so clueless sometimes.

Logan is coming back from the bar with our drinks when I spot them. Taking my drink from him I whisper, "Don't look now but M & S are heading this way." He looks over his shoulder and groans.

"Ladies, how lovely to see you." Logan's voice drips with sarcasm. Both of them give him the finger.

"We're here to be with Tahlia and Georgia, you can scoot, this will be girl talk only." Logan laughs at Miller and stays where he is grabbing my hand. "Oh, it's like that is it, you two are a thing now?"

"None of your business and I will stay wherever I bloody well please."

"Yeah, big boy, I got that." She turns to me and says, "How's things Tahlia?"

Georgia pipes up, "Things were fine until you two showed up. Stop ruining our night. And for the record, stop ruining our lunch times too."

"Well aren't we being a bitch, Georgia. Just being friendly that's all. Come on Scarlett, we know when we're not wanted."

I breathe out a sigh of relief when they're gone. The last people I want to be friends with is those two. "Thanks Georgia, let's hope they finally leave us alone."

"I wouldn't bank on it. Come on, it's time to dance." She grabs my hand and we head to the dance floor where we stay for most the night. We don't mention Miller and Scarlett again.

LOGAN and I are in my room.

"It's pink."

This being the first time he has been to my place and meeting my mum, I'm not surprised he's commenting. "When my parents divorced, mum and I moved here. There was no money to fix anything up, so ... yes, it's pink." And not your average pink either, it's a bright, hot pink, something a Barbie-loving girl would love. *Me?* Not so much. Give me blue any day.

"Your mum seems nice," he says sitting at my desk.

"She's cool. It's only her and me, so ..."

"I guess so," he shrugs. "Umm, I had fun tonight. Enjoyed the way Georgia dealt with M & S."

I pull off my jumper throwing it on the floor and place myself on his lap helping him to take off his parker. "Well maybe they'll get the hint this time. I still don't believe their crap about breaking up with their idiot boyfriends, why else would they want to be friends with us?"

"Yep, definitely a James Bond-like spy thing going on there." He smiles and kisses my neck. Then he starts to pull up my t-shirt.

He's staring. "What?"

"I'm admiring the view. You are beautiful."

The blush starts from my chest and reaches my face in seconds. I kiss his lips with a passion as strong as the blush, "You ain't so bad yourself, Logan Shipley."

He holds onto me and stands up, kissing me as he guides us to my bed. It looks like this night is going to be even more fun.

GEORGIA and I are sitting with Manuel and Aaron under the Jacaranda when we see M & S heading our way. Do they not understand we don't want to be friends?

"Geeks, nice to see you." This is Miller and then she gives us the finger as she and Scarlett walk past us towards the oval.

"Well, what do you know, they did get the hint." I high-five Georgia.

We tell the boys about being hassled by those two and how glad we are they seem to have given up finally. They laugh too and then we move on to discussing what we're thinking of doing when school finishes, in only two months' time. "I'm thinking of nursing or maybe pharmacy, although I need super high grades to do pharmacy."

"I haven't thought about it yet, Tahlia," answers Manuel. I find this surprising given the timing of making a decision is right on us. "I might take a gap year because I have no idea what I want to do. Maybe graphics, maybe finance? No idea at all."

"Logan and Jack are thinking about a gap year too."

"I know, I've spoken to them about it. The difference is they both have an idea of what they want to do, Logan will do something in the building trade like his father. And Jack, he wants to pursue acting. I mean, how good has he been in the school plays? His singing voice isn't bad either."

What Manuel is saying is true, Jack is a born performer and has played the lead in the last two school plays.

"Well, I have two chosen careers – journalism or chef."

We all look at Georgia with surprise. "Those two couldn't be more different!"

"I know, Aaron. But I enjoy writing and I love cooking. So I haven't decided yet."

"Having eaten your cookies and cakes, I'd say go for being a chef, or a pastry chef at least," says Aaron. "Ooh, can't wait to see a cookbook authored by you."

"Hmmm, that's not a bad idea. Combine my love of writing with baking. Hey Tahlia, how are you going to cope if Logan is away for a year? He seems serious about travelling."

"Well that will be interesting. I'm not thinking that far ahead yet, we're having a good time for now."

I think about Logan with my body reacting, I like the way he makes me feel. He and I have many things in common, he makes me laugh too. It may have taken him some time to ask me out, but now we are dating and I am happy being with him. He seems as taken by me as I am by him, always attentive, protective without being controlling and he makes me feel loved and safe. And I'm dating a magical, that is so cool.

Manuel is still talking about the gap year when a chime signalling the end of lunch takes us away from our chat and we each head to our respective classrooms. *How am I going to feel when Logan is gone?*

FIFTEEN

Logan
  The Cast Comes Off

I'M SITTING at the police station waiting for Constable Jane Pathe when she walks towards me and notices my cast with all the signatures.

"Hi Logan, you're popular, your cast is full of graffiti." She points to my leg, "Thanks for coming in."

"It comes off in a couple of weeks and I can't wait," I say as I follow her to the interview room. I recount what I can remember about the night I sustained this injury and then ask if anything will happen to the bullies. I also apologise for not coming in sooner, studying takes up a lot of my time.

"As there were no other witnesses, it's your word against theirs. We can caution them and keep them in our sights, but that's all I'm afraid. What I don't understand is how did you get away from them?"

I hate that I need to lie about this, but I tell her what my parents and I had agreed to. "A group of three coming from a nearby party scared Donovan and Parker off and then called an ambulance for me. They waited until I was safe with the arrival of the paramedics but I don't remember their names."

"Would you be able to identify them if we find something in the CCTV footage?"

"I could try, but I really don't remember them." Shit, I hadn't thought of the street surveillance cameras, they'll show what happened and the goblins. I start to fidget with nerves. Footage ... shit!

We finish up the interview with me promising to contact her again if I remember anything else and she wishes me well with my studies.

I'm walking out of the station and with a shaking hand I take my phone out of my pocket. Calling Mum I ask her about the CCTV cameras.

"Oh don't worry about that, Logan. Leafia and her goblins can't be seen on those cameras, they're not human."

Relief washes over me. "Ok, that's fine, whew. But the three men won't show up either, they don't exist. What do we say about that?"

"Hmm, you're right. Let's discuss that tonight with your father. I'm sure we can come up with something."

Later that night we do come up with a plan to say the camera might be faulty but if the police dispute that, then we have no explanation. We keep discussing this and come up with a feeble plan to take the police in another direction taking the focus off the footage.

In the end we didn't have to worry because the video showed a message 'video loss due to network failure' when the police checked. Constable Pathe had called my dad to let him know and so no action against the two bullies would be taken, all the video showed was me talking to Donovan and Parker and then went to the message.

"Obviously this is the handy work of Leafia."

I look at Dad and smile. She and her fellow goblins are turning out to be quite an asset for us.

MUM HAS TAKEN me to our local doctor as I can't drive. Getting this cast off will mean I can drive again, which I have missed. With my right leg out of action, my independence took a knock.

I hobble into the doctor's office without the crutches, we had already handed those back to the hospital. "Hi Logan, sit up on the bed please," asks my doctor after I enter his room. He takes out a small blue and grey saw with a circular blade. "Try not to move while I do this."

I feel the vibration as he cuts into the plaster cast, what a weird sensation of tingles up my leg. It doesn't take long and all I want to do is rub my shin. "Let me check how it's healed. It looks ok." He lifts my ankle and pushes his finger on the break, "Does this hurt?"

"A little," I answer. "It's itchy more than hurting." I look down and see the dry skin, "Is my ankle skinnier now?"

"Well yes, you've lost some muscle mass but I'll give you exercises that will help. Also, moisturiser will be good. Often. Come back and see me if you notice anything unusual like swelling or redness."

"Thanks doctor." I stretch out my hand to shake his and walk out to where mum is sitting. She also thanks the doctor, "I'll keep an eye on him and make sure he does his exercises." Having broken her leg at a young age, she knew about them. She had mentioned them to me on our way to the surgery.

I look towards her with a quizzical look, what am I a baby? Of course I'll do the exercises.

WITH THE CAST having been taken off last Friday afternoon, it was great to walk into school with only a slight limp, the exercises won't kick in for weeks yet. It's good not to be so itchy too, I've never used so much moisturiser.

I hear a few "welcome backs" and "hey, Logan" with a thumbs up and am glad to be back here, not that I missed school so much, but I did miss seeing my friends. Chloe was the only one able to come and visit while I was stuck at home.

Lunchtime comes around before I know it and I look forward to seeing everyone, especially Tahlia, I always want to see her. I'm the last one to arrive at our spot. She comes up and hugs me for what seems like a long time. "Nice, thanks Tahlia, but you saw me on Friday."

"I know, but you still had the cast on then. Now look, you're walking almost like a normal person. That deserves a bigger hug."

We all laugh, with Chloe adding, "Ah, do you feel naked without it?"

"No way, I couldn't wait to get it off. Now I can scratch as much as I like." I bend and scratch a spot, there are some itchy spots still bothering me. "So, not long now before we finish school and get on with our lives."

"Except me, I have another year, remember? And so does Tahlia"

"Except you two, sorry Chloe, my bad."

"How are we going to cope next year without you guys?"

"Our weekends will be full of get togethers. Don't forget none of us will see each other every day after November."

That will be a strange feeling, after years of seeing each other five days a week, we will have to wait for the weekends to stay in touch.

We all nod and stay quiet as we contemplate what our lives will look like in the next few years. Continuing to talk, we discuss our thoughts and ideas for the next year. I'm closer to deciding I will take a gap year, Jack has already decided.

"Yes, I want to travel and Manuel here is coming along too."

Manuel looks at Jack smiling. "Yeah, I have no idea what to do, so with the money from my job at Maccas, I'm joining Jack, and maybe you too, Logan."

"Great, I'm almost there with the decision, I want to see how the exams go and then check out courses available with what I get. But it's more yes than no."

As the bell goes, we boys keep talking about where to visit until we split and head to our classrooms. I smile at the fact Manuel is taking a year off too. He and Jack, well … I'm happy for them.

Jack had told me about the threats Matt had thrown at them and how Manuel had stood up to his bullying. Jack has never made a secret of him being gay, but Manuel has only recently come out. He has had trouble with his family, which he doesn't like talking about. That anger at his family probably fuelled his outburst at Matt, and if I'd been in that situation, I would have done a lot worse. Matt is more trouble than he is worth.

SIXTEEN

Donovan
    The Bullies Don't Stop

PARKER and I are at our gang's headquarters with our girls. Miller told us about the geek girls not wanting them around. "So you can't give us any intel?" She and Scarlett are sitting on the torn old lounge, with us opposite them on the rickety office chairs.

"Only from a distance."

"Ok, then we need to keep a closer eye on Logan and Jacky, make sure we know what they're doing. We need to catch them doing some magical shit."

Parker, who rarely comments, speaks. "We've seen those animals a lot now, why haven't we thought to take a photo or video of them?"

Miller and Scarlett shrug and I look at Parker surprised. "Good point, Parks. Even more reason to watch them, we need evidence of them changing into their animals. Now, you two," I continue as I wave my finger towards the girls, "keep tracking them, especially outside of school. The best time for us is when it's just the two of 'em."

"There are a lot of geeks, why do you target those two?"

"Apart from them being annoying shits, Scarlett, they have something to do with the animals. I know it. The animals only appear when they're around. Oh, and that other one, Chloe, when she's around that white fluffy thing turns up. And the three of them, their human form, disappear. Nah, something's not right."

We keep talking about the possibility of magic or some other sort of occult crap happening. We decide without proof there is not much we can do. Our mission now is to get that proof. And I make it my mission to defend our girls, Tahlia and Georgia can't treat them like that and get away with it.

We're about to leave when Matt comes in. "Hey, buddy."

"Hi."

"Hmm, talkative today huh? You ok?"

"No, Don, I'm not. Super pissed off with my family." I explain what happened when I found Jack and Manuel together.

The four of them stare at me for some time before Donovan speaks again, "Well that's not the way a son should be treated. Stick with us, Matt, we'll show your brother Jack and his squeeze just what we think of them. But first, we need to deal with our the issue of our girls being treated like shit."

I SEE them walk out of the shopping centre. Parks and I walk towards them. I become even angrier when I see Logan and Jack shake their heads. "Nice to see you both, too. What's with going to the cops? We were only talking to you that night Logan." He seems to take a minute before speaking, had he forgotten about the other night?"

"Not everything is about you, Don. I went to see the police about something else, none of your business what it was."

"That's bullshit. You and that lady cop are chummy, aren't ya?"

"Listen, there are people around, let's not make a scene."

"Shut up, Jacky. Not talkin' to you yet. Tell me what you told the police, Logan cause they've been sniffing around us and the others in our gang."

"How is that our problem? Did you or any of your gang members have anything to do with the convenience store robberies? You know the police are still investigating those."

Before I can answer him, Tahlia and Georgia walk out of the centre and join us. This is convenient. "Lovely to see you ladies. Just the ones we wanted to speak to as well. Miller and Scarlett are a bit disappointed."

The girls look at each other, Tahlia speaks. "So you're still friends even though you all split up?"

"What? They're our girlfriends and we're here defending them. No one treats our girls like you two did. We're not pleased and there will be consequences."

"Oh, stop threatening us, Don. You and Parks go back to your gang and keep robbing shops, that's what you're good at, obviously. Come on, let's go, I've had enough of these two." Logan turns towards Jack and the girls as they head to the bus stop.

Parker starts after us but I call him back. "Leave it, Parks. We'll deal with them another time, next time at night when there is no one around. I know Logan spoke to the cops about us, otherwise why did they come to the head-quarters yesterday?"

I WATCH her as she enters my room after going to the bathroom. Her body is slim, her chestnut hair flows down her naked back as she sits on my bed and starts dressing. Miller is my girl and I'm still pissed with those geek girls treating her and Scarlett like they are beneath them. She's dressed and is standing up about to leave. "I will do something about those two, will teach them a lesson."

She turns looking towards me, "I gotta go, but like I said earlier, just leave it. With the cops sniffing around the gang, I think you should lay low for now. We knew they weren't going to believe the lie about us not being together."

"Yeah, but ..."

"Don, leave it alone." Her face reddens with anger, "I'm going to work. Promise me you won't do anything stupid."

I look at her as she heads towards the door, she is right, it is dangerous with the cops sniffing around. But I'm glad to have given those geeks a scare, they'll keep looking over their shoulders.

My stomach rumbles so I pull on my shorts and head to the kitchen hoping there will be something decent to eat. While I head there, I hatch a plan on how to deal with the geeks that doesn't involve being physical.

A PHOTO OPPORTUNITY happens out of the blue a few days later. We're at the park and across the road from the derelict house when something catches Parker's eye. "Hey Don, look, there's people coming out of that dump."

Looking over I see he's right. "Quick, get your phone

out, what the hell are they doing in the place? And what, there's at least a dozen of 'em. Wait, taking a random photo of people coming out of that dump isn't enough to convince people magicals exist. We need to get them to do magic in front of us." With this we both run over the road.

"Hello there boys." This comes from a short woman with wayward hair dressed in something out of the 1950s.

"What you all doin' in that old place? Isn't it dangerous going in there?"

"Well, actually, it's none of your business what we are doing, young man, I was just being friendly. Now out of our way, we all have places to be. You two stop loitering around here, this property is off bounds."

"Off bounds? Obviously not to you. Don't tell us where we can and can't be. Right, Parks, let's go check out what's so interesting in this place." We push the gate and head towards the front door having already taken some photos.

"Err, I wouldn't if I were you." I look back to see the woman close her eyes and next thing there are two Dobermans growling at us. Where the hell did they come from?" We both step back as they bear their teeth. Parks is continuing to take photos when the dogs jump at us. We hot foot it out the gate, slamming it shut. The woman quietens the two dogs down with just a hand gesture. Hmm, the obedient pooches they are.

The group is murmuring between themselves. "Excuse us, but what the hell just happened? Those dogs seem to have appeared as if by magic."

The woman and a man I now recognise as Logan's father, walk towards us. He speaks, "Donovan, be a good boy and head home before you get hurt."

"Edward, right? Edward Shipley, something is fishy

about you and your son. And now we have photos to prove it." I pull on Parker's arm and we run.

An hour later, it's dark and Parks and I are at my place. I don't remember how we got here. "Weren't we at that old derelict house just now?"

"What are you talkin' about? We've been in your room all afternoon. Come on, it's your turn." I look at my computer and see we're playing a video game. By the score, we have been playing for hours. Then I look at my phone checking photos, I haven't taken any since ages ago.

"Parks, hand me your phone." He does so and as I check, I only see photos of him and Scarlett, one of his dick being somewhere it shouldn't be. Gagging, I give him back his phone and keep playing, obviously my mind is playing tricks on me.

SEVENTEEN

Jack
   The Geeks Arrive

FRIDAY AFTERNOON and Manuel and I are waiting for Logan and Aaron, they're at the fish 'n' chip place getting us chips. I'm starving, all this studying makes me hungry. They're taking their time, but I'm not surprised, that shop is always busy, especially on a Friday afternoon when students are ravenous after a week of school.

We're talking about our gap year trip, both of us are excited about having this adventure together. I hear a branch break and turn to face a punch from Donovan. Manuel is dragged off his seat by Parker.

I'm on the ground, my nose bleeding. Donovan is shaking his hand, he's hurt it. "What's this all about?" I cough up some blood and wipe my nose with my shirt sleeve.

Donovan stands over me but I'm focusing on Manuel, Parker and he are in a fist fight. "Look at me Jacky, I'm talking to you. So, I hear your family treats Matt with disrespect ..." Matt is behind Donovan. "We are here to set the record straight."

Matt looks at me with a weird smile and kicks my shin, "Did you think I was going to let you and Manuel get away with that sort of treatment. You've got our olds wrapped around your finger, bro. And I don't like it."

Manuel is next to me helping me up, I see Parker writhing on the floor holding his hand. "Your friend is injured, Don, he needs help." Donovan goes over and talks to Parker then calls someone on his phone. If it's backup, we're in real trouble.

Matt and Manuel are having a screaming match, so while everyone is distracted, I head behind I tree and transform. I attack Matt, grabbing hold of his ankle.

He easily shakes me off, "You don't scare me, you poor excuse for a dog." Manuel grabs Matt in a head lock and I yap a high-pitched bark, bearing my teeth then jumping and grabbing my brother's hand. Teeth marks bleed as he screams in pain.

Donovan kicks me flying as I let go of Matt's hand. I'm thrown into bushes but can see Logan and Aaron running towards us. There are other geeks following them. We have backup.

Logan is behind the bush where I'm laying still winded, he transforms telling me to stay put.

Aaron is dealing with Parker, Logan as the Maine Coon, attacks Donovan who lashes out furiously missing Logan every time. He rubs his legs, blood coming from the many scratches Logan has inflicted. Then he suddenly moves towards Jack, who has transformed back after catching his breath.

Donovan is about the hit him again when Matt grabs

hold of his hand. "Stop, you've done enough damage, look his nose is swollen."

"You protecting your brother now, Matt? What the hell? You wanted us to teach him and Manuel a lesson, now you're going soft."

"Jack's nose is probably broken, Parker's injured too. We've done enough damage."

"That wasn't the deal, Matty-boy, you said you wanted them pummelled and not be recognisable. You can't have a foot in both camps, either you're with us or you're not."

When he finishes talking, Cole and Maddox appear on the scene. Cole has his trusty cricket bat with him. The geeks rally around the four of us, phones in hand filming.

Logan speaks to the four bullies, Donovan holding onto Parker who's hand is wrapped in someone's jumper. "Do we really need to post this on social media? Aren't you and your gang already in enough trouble?" The geeks had been filming all of what had happened, this time the footage showed the fighting, something the police will be interested in seeing.

Matt whispers something into Donovan's ear. "Hmm, seems our boy wants us to show some compassion but this will only happen if Jack and Manuel show compassion to Matt, treat him with respect and we'll consider this ended. Well, Jacky, what do you say?"

I speak to Manuel, whispering that I think we should agree. Then we both turn towards the bullies nodding. Matt looks at us both laughing, a maniacal laugh if ever I heard one. I've said it before and I'll say it again, my brother is heading for trouble with friends like these thugs.

My dad arrives after Donovan and his crew have left. He looks at my face with my eyes and nose now so swollen I can hardly see and shakes his head. "Again, Jack. I can't believe those thugs are always finding an excuse to hurt you."

"As usual, we were minding our own business, Mr Sterling."

"I know, Manuel, you guys aren't to blame. Where's Matt?" He looks around finding only the four of us here.

"He took off with them, Dad. He is so pissed at us."

"Tell me something I don't know, Jack. But for now let's get you to emergency and have your nose fixed."

I'M the talk of the school playground again. Everyone is telling both Manuel and me how they wish that gang would just disappear and leave us in peace. The fact Matt was involved this time has them doubly angry. Matt is avoiding everyone by staying in the library as often as possible. Some students have 'accidentally' bumped him while walking past where he is sitting, the finger being used often too. Matt is not popular at all now, not that he was before this anyway.

The disappointment I feel of having a brother who won't listen to reason is driving me insane. Our parents grounded him yet again, but I can't see how this will help when he's still keeping in touch with the gang. He did say sorry about what happened, he hadn't wanted me to get injured badly again, just given a warning. "That's why I stopped Donovan going any further," he had said. Our dad had responded with a barrage of anger, "You know that gang is dangerous and you still insist on being a part of it. What part of you puny brain doesn't get that? We're all trying to stop the gang doing any more damage and you go and do this, I'm livid, you are a fool." He didn't stop there, our mum had to calm him down and had sent Matt to bed.

The day after when we were both home after school, Matt apologised to me. My face ached and I looked like I'd been bashed into a wall, so I wasn't in any state to listen to his fake apology. My swollen cheeks, nose and puffy eyes the size of walnuts were enough to keep my anger seething.

"Really, you're sorry?" My words come out slightly muffled due to my injuries, Donovan was right on top of me when he hit me. "I've had enough of your antics and the way you got involved in my personal life, it's just unacceptable. My love life is no one else's business and you will know that if and when you ever fall in love."

He looks up at me from his place on the lounge, I'm standing up not wanting to be near him. "Jack, you're my brother, I wasn't going to let them hurt you too much. And can't you see how they respect me, Donovan listened."

I laugh, "Gee, thanks bro, after this was done to me you stopped them. Look at my face." I start to walk out of the lounge, "You want respect, then how about giving us some? The way you treat our family, you're disappointing all of us." I wave my hand in disgust, "Leave me the hell alone and if you ever try to hurt Manuel and I again, you won't be forgiven. Can't wait to leave for Europe and get away from you."

I walk into my room slamming the door. How did I end up with such a jerk of a brother.

EIGHTEEN

Logan
　The Return of Cyberbullying

THE PARK IS DESERTED besides us, although the out-dated park equipment is rarely used anyway, the chances of a parent with their kid using it are slim. It's late afternoon, so it's a bit cooler. I look around at all the geeks chatting before we start our meeting. We have become a group of good friends who look out for each other, this makes me proud because I had something to do with this. Thanks to my dad for starting a revolution against bullying.

There is only a week of school left, all exams are done and this is something we're all happy about. But there is something we're not happy with and it's the reason for this meeting, the bullies have ramped up the cyberbullying again. They began with Tahlia and Georgia, using AI images of them in compromising positions. Then each of us was targeted, some with images, some with text and emojis. We've all had enough.

"Constable Pathe has been informed. The police will be checking the gang's headquarters and, with a warrant, they will look for evidence. We all know it is this gang that is doing this, no one else we know has a reason to target us in this way." I look around and see everyone agrees with me. Fielding questions, I answer with as much information as I know. "The police found the IP addresses last time, I'm sure they will again. The best thing to do is ignore the posts, send them to our group chat and I'll pass them onto the police."

"Do we delete them? I can't stand to see them in my feed." This question is from one of the new Year 7 kids, a year at high school and he is having to deal with this crap.

"You can, yes. If police need anything more from your phones, they have ways of finding what they need. I ask all of you to be diligent during the holidays and call one of us," I point to myself, Jack, Manuel and Aaron, "if you are worried about anything. We've been through this once before and we can help. Thanks for coming everyone, enjoy the rest of your afternoon." I hear a few 'thanks' and some of them clap. I am pleased to be able to help and hope to one day not have to deal with bullies like Donovan, Parker and their stupid gang.

TAHLIA IS WEEPING, actually no ... she is sobbing uncontrollably. Her body shakes with each draining sob and I don't know what to do to help. She had called me to come to her place because of yet another barrage of disgusting posts using hers and Georgia's faces. We're in her bedroom, she is pacing. "Have you told you mum about this? Isn't she worried about you?"

"No, oh Jesus, no! If she saw these she would take my phone away and probably ground me."

"What? This isn't your fault, Tahlia. I thought you said she was cool?"

"Yeah, well, tell her it's not my fault. She is cool, mostly. Just not about tech stuff." She snuffles and rubs her nose with her wrist. I hand her a tissue from her bedside table. "Thanks." Blowing her nose she continues, "Your parents are the cool ones, I'm sure your dad can help."

She is beginning to compose herself now, although her face is puffy and red, her eyes rimmed and swollen from crying. I have to do something serious, I can't see her suffer like this. "Dad can help and I think the three of us should go to the police. Maybe ask Georgia if she wants to come too. This can't keep happening and you can't keep doing this to yourself."

"Oh, Logan, thank you." She slumps into my arms and I go into protection mode, I love her too much to let her keep suffering. As I soothe her anger seethes through me, those bullies are going to get what's coming.

DAD, Tahlia and I are sitting in the interrogation room at the police station. I seem to be frequenting this place a bit too much. Georgia had declined to come siting she is too embarrassed to talk about it. This is another reason why we had to come to the police, Tahlia and Georgia are victims in all this, they shouldn't be blaming themselves.

"We're a step ahead of you Logan, we have a warrant to search the gang's headquarters this week. Tahlia, I'm so sorry this is happening to you, but whoever is doing this they are doing it to hurt Logan as well as you." Constable Pathe sits opposite us with a steaming mug of what I assume is coffee, it doesn't smell like coffee, though. I had overheard Constable Pathe talk about this beverage that tastes like bitter dishwater. Not sure why she bothers drinking it.

"Well, they're doing a good job because this is hurting both of us and Georgia, as well as others in our group."

"I can see that, one look at your faces tells me how upset you both are."

"We're all upset," interjects my dad, "we know it's that gang doing this again. We parents have had enough too and we want something done about it."

"I understand, Mr Shipley. Having the warrant will help us but without evidence we can't go accusing the gang of anything."

Dad stands up, anger swirls on his face, "It's obvious the gang is doing this, who else in this town holds such grudges."

I put my hand on dad's arm to stop him talking again, "Ok, thanks Constable, we'll leave you to it. Please let us know if you need our help or if you find out anything more." Dad harrumphs but keeps quiet.

"Of course, Logan, we'll be in touch if we need you. Thank you for coming in, I'll see you all out."

When we reach the car, Dad asks, "Why didn't you let me talk in there, I wanted to know if they had any leads."

"They have a warrant now, this will help in finding out what the gang is hiding at their headquarters. There was no need to take up more of the constable's time."

"Hmm, ok, fair enough." Looking at Dad's face, I know he isn't impressed but it was time to let the police get to work on this.

When we're driving away from the station I think about the damage those idiot gang members are doing. Looking out the window at the suburban streets I know so well, I wish we weren't dealing with these bullies and I'm hoping I won't have to go back to the police station too many more times.

NINETEEN

Jack
Matt and The Gang

I'M in my bedroom and need a break, I've been studying all day. I'm surprised to see it's past nine and my stomach lets out a loud groan – *feed me!* Jeez, studying makes me hungry. I head to the kitchen and hear my parents chatting in the lounge. I pop my head in.

"Hey you, how's the studying?"

"Making me hungry, any leftovers Mum?"

"Open the fridge, there's plenty in there. Matt didn't come home for dinner."

"Again? What the hell does he get up to every night? Not that I miss him, my face is only just looking normal again."

Dad speaks with concern, "We thought you might be able to tell us. Whenever we try to speak to him we receive a surly reply to mind our own business. Although he's probably with those idiots at the gang's headquarters."

"Give me a minute to get some food, then I'll come and sit with you." I scrounge through the fridge and find some cold chicken, that will do.

Walking into the lounge, I sit comfortably on a lounge chair and chomp on a chicken leg. Once I've chewed enough of it, I say, "He was fine for that little bit after Logan's birthday, then suddenly he started being a dick again and being part of the gang. Although, he hasn't been in my room again, so that's something."

Mum laughs, "He wouldn't want to do that, you gave him a huge fright last time. But what is he up to now?"

I place the chewed bone onto my plate, the chicken hit the spot so with my stomach satisfied, I answer, "I'm not sure but more than likely with those gang members. I'll ask around and see if anyone knows or has seen him around at night. Most people hate him so will tell me whatever I want to know." Before either of my parents can respond, we hear the front door. *Well what do you know, my jerk of a brother has decided to come home.*

Mum stands to go and greet him but he runs up the stairs two by two and whispers a quick "Hi." I can hear his footsteps quicken up the stairs.

"Matt Sterling, get your arse down here. What's this coming home without greeting us?"

Matt is at the top of the stairs and whines, "Ah, Dad, I'm bushed. Going to bed."

"I said get down here, that's an order!"

Dad's tightened jaw and flaring nostrils show his anger, there is going to be another confrontation, which are all too regular in this house. I sit uncomfortably waiting for what will happen when Matt comes into the lounge room. I don't have to wait long. Then mum is next to dad trying to calm him down.

"You have no right to be out every night like this, Matt. We warned you when this happened last time. Explain what the hell you are doing out this late at your age. You do realise you are still a minor."

Matt has his head hanging, his face bland and bored when he looks up. "Just out with friends, what's wrong with that?"

"And who are these friends? Do we know them? Not those gang idiots?" Dad is shaking off Mum's hand and moves closer to Matt, who doesn't even flinch. I'm shaking with fear, Dad is intimidating when he's angry.

"Mates from school, you know some of them. Can I go to bed now?"

"No, you may not go to bed. Not until you tell us what's going on with you, if something is going on, you need to tell us so we can help."

Matt looks at Dad scowling, "Nothing's going on. I go out and enjoy time with my friends, is that a crime?"

"Don't you give me that look, young man. I'm your father, show some respect."

"I'm telling you the truth, look here's a photo of us," he shows us a photo of him and two other boys.

"You took that tonight?"

"Yes Dad, I did. We were mucking around and thought it was funny.

"Hmm, off you go to bed now and in the morning we will discuss you and your behaviour towards us, things are going to change or else."

I can see Dad's veins pulsing in his neck. Matt is in huge trouble and this gives me great pleasure.

. . .

DAYS later I'm telling everyone about what happened with Matt. He's grounded from going out at night, even on weekends, for a month. "The idiot was going to that gang's headquarters again, apparently they promised him all sorts of things if he spilled on us."

"What *things*?" asks Logan.

"Money, tech stuff, a new iPhone. And he believed them. He had been telling them of our whereabouts, which is how they found us all the time, but at least he did stop at telling them about us magicals."

"What an idiot. As if they were going to give him that stuff, where were they going to get it all, let alone give him money. And not ratting out about our magic, well he's smarter than I thought."

"My olds were furious yet again and I don't blame them for grounding him. It was only a matter of time before he did spill our secret."

We keep talking about my idiot brother and how living with him being tied to the house like this is not great. He's in an even worse mood this time. Matt doesn't talk to us, stays in his room, and is generally being a dick.

"He has always been a dick, Jack. The older he gets, the worse he is. That gang has truly brainwashed him," adds Manuel.

"How awful for you both," says Tahlia, "And Jack, what a horrible thing to go home to."

"Yeah, it's not fun but I'm happy to avoid him, just like I did last time. Somehow I don't think this will stop him going back once the month is up either, he can be stupid like that." Everyone nods because they all know how Matt behaves, he really has a chip on his shoulder.

Two days after his grounding, Matt runs out of the front door, slamming it. Dad is after him in a flash and drags him back into the kitchen. Mum and I are clearing the breakfast dishes.

"Where the hell were you going?"

"I'm late for school, I have an early running session this morning. Let me go or I'll miss the training."

"And you couldn't tell us about this training session?"

"Can't you just trust me. You've told me not to go to the gang's headquarters and I haven't but for f-sake let me lead my life."

"You watch your language young man, let me get my keys and I'll drop you at school." Matt stays where he is waiting for dad, his glare towards me makes me want to pummel him again.

When they're gone I ask Mum, "He wants us to trust him more? He keeps going back to that gang and causing trouble for all of us."

She looks at me with her face calm save for a small smirk, "I wouldn't trust your brother to do the right thing. Sure, he wasn't lying this morning, but how many times has he lied in the past?" The look of disappointment on her face makes me sad for her, it must be tough being a parent of such an idiot. I know how tough it is being his older brother. Not that I had much respect for him before, but now it's all gone.

I nod and head up to my room, picking up my bag I head back downstairs. "Bye Mum."

"Bye darling, see you this afternoon."

I head to the school bus stop wondering if there will ever be a day when my brother isn't a dick, or worse, gets into real trouble that involves gaol time.

TWENTY

Edward
It's Time to Step Up

I'M at The Arms with Noel, we're waiting for our wives to come back from the ladies so we can have dessert. We'd met for an early dinner before going to the movies. "You should have seen poor Tahlia." I'm explaining to him what happened, "her face was full of shame and Logan showed me the posts, they were disgusting and brutal. And she wasn't the only one targeted, other geeks were too."

"But she bore the brunt of this abuse, right?"

"Yes, her and Georgia. Whoever is doing this ... we're sure it's the gang, they want to hurt both Logan and the two girls. They have achieved this, unfortunately. Logan is beside himself seeing Tahlia so hurt."

"Poor kids. This makes me so mad, especially as I did things too, not as bad but I was a bully back in the day." He is about to keep talking when Sally and Hannah return.

I wait for them to sit down. "Yes you were, but you

came good. These idiots just keep going, targeting and humiliating our kids and their school friends. Many are young Year 7 kids and they have no idea how to deal with this."

"Are you two talking about Tahlia and all the cyberbullying. It's awful."

"More than awful, Sally. Edward, we need to put a stop to this. Let the police do their bit, but maybe we should give them another scare, maybe you use your skills again?" Noel is looking at me with determination.

Hannah sighs, "Every time we use our magic to target a big group like this gang we run the risk of being exposed. We need to be careful."

I understand what she is talking about. "Yes, Hannah, the larger the group, the more chance multiple people will see us and work out what's happening. It makes it harder for us to erase everyone's memory. We just have to miss one and ..."

"I don't want to think about that happening."

"I'm with you Hannah. How's Matt doing?" asks Sally.

"Noel and she look at each other, both despondent. "Well, he's been home at night, so that's a good thing. We take turns in checking he doesn't sneak out, but then he can always text Donovan whenever he wants."

"Taking his phone off him again is not an option, I suppose? You'd have to ban him for life." We all nod as Sally continues, "Now, what are we having for dessert?" Then she reminds us we have a movie to see by pointing to her watch.

We keep talking about Matt and how a counsellor may help until it's time to go to the cinemas. Watching the movie takes my mind off Matt and his antics until Noel badgers me again to do something to scare the bullies as we're walking out to go home. I promise him I'll speak to other committee members. "We'll work something out, Noel, leave it with me."

I'M at the A-Alliance house with the other committee members as well as Leafia. We're discussing what we can do about this gang. We already know the police have confiscated computers and other things from the gang headquarters but we haven't heard anything further. We are seated around the large kitchen table listening to Leafia's ideas.

"We goblins see all sorts when we patrol the streets at night, being careful not to be seen, of course." She continues telling us how most nights are quiet and they don't have to help too many non-magicals, but Friday and Saturday nights are another matter. "That gang, they are relentless and target anyone, no one is safe on those nights, especially when the gang members are stoned."

"Yes, I bet that makes them even more dangerous," says Ester. "So, your idea is to scare them again using Logan, Jack and Chloe in their animal forms being more vicious than usual and with Edward's paralysing spell. A stronger version maybe? We can target them at their headquarters?"

"Unless anyone has a better idea. If the animals can keep them all in one place, their headquarters being the easiest, then Edward can cast his spell showing them what their horrific future will look like. We goblins can then cast the memory spell on them once they have seen enough, probably towards the morning. This is best done on a night they have a meeting." The committee members all nod and murmur their agreement.

I reply to Leafia, "Sounds good to me, but Leafia, you can't erase all of the memory of their future, some has to remain so they learn from it. And I can help by bringing back Milly the Cat, I'll be able to help the other animals. It will be nice to have the ginger around again."

"That's a good point. We will tweak the spell so they remember their future but not what the animals do and you casting the spell. I thought you retired Milly the Cat, Edward?"

"I have, but this is an emergency, no reason I can't help out in my animal form. And Leafia, make it a vivid memory to give them a jolt each time, they have to be spooked into wondering what the hell is going on. This might take the focus off them doing all this horrible stuff." I am so hopeful this plan will work.

We continue talking about Donovan and Parker's attempt to take photos of committee members coming out of the A-Alliance house. "We were lucky yet again that the memory spell worked on them both, and what a brilliant idea to take them both back to Donovan's house, Leafia. With the added genius of speeding up a video game to make it look like they'd been there all afternoon. Brilliant!

THE NIGHT of the gang's next main meeting is a week away and we're ready for them. The police have yet to release any details of their raid and we are sure this meeting will be all about the raid. This will mean most of their members will attend, which is perfect for us. The more gang members we can scare, the better.

Leafia and her goblins have changed the paralysing spell enough so the gang members will remember their dismal futures if they continue down this destructive path. I have tested the spell on Noel and it works fine, he remembers what he sees of his future while paralysed. And his future looks fine, which is a good thing.

I'm now looking forward to the night along with Logan, Jack, Chloe and the goblins, we now feel like we're doing something that will help everyone affected by the stupid antics of this gang.

I'm at the door of the gang headquarters with Logan, Jack and Chloe. They have transformed into their animal forms and are waiting for me to allow them inside. I check through a cracked side window and see the members are all looking towards Cole and Maddox who are on the makeshift stage. It's time to pounce.

I watch on as Logan and Jack, as the Maine Coon and the Jack Russell, run up to the stage and attack the two head gang members. Cole is swearing with vigour while trying to get the Maine Coon off his ankle. Logan has his teeth firmly imbedded. Maddox has been bitten by Jack, blood spurting from his calf and I laugh watching him, as the Jack Russel, yapping fiercely, his bark is more like a squeak but at least he's annoying them.

I make my way in when I see the other members try to catch the animals, Chloe, as the Ragdoll, being caught by Donovan. I transform into the ginger, Milly the Cat, just as she wriggles out of Donovan's arms giving him what look like major scratches as she scrambles away. I do more damage as Milly to a few others, namely Alex and Callum, who have been quiet lately, this must be their first time back at headquarters. They gave the geeks hell and then added Donovan and Parker to their arsenal. I take pleasure in giving them both severe scratches on their legs and arms. Blood and eerie screams of pain ooze around the headquarters. There is a frenzy of gang members trying to catch us, but we are too quick for all of them.

Transforming back, the paralysing spell is cast and I target as many members as I can at one time. The animals are making a good time of escaping from the members and soon I have paralysed all of them. It looks to me like there are at least thirty members here tonight. Walking up to the four gang members on stage – Cole, Maddox, Donovan and Parker, I see they all have multiple injuries. Alex and Callum have definite fear in their eyes and follow me around with them. We animals have done our job well, now it's my turn to make sure the paralysis spell works for long enough.

All the gang members are staring at the 'movie' showing on the old stage curtains, it's showing their futures. I enjoy seeing the fear in their eyes. We're all back in our human form and continue to stay and keep watch, I want to make sure the spell doesn't wear off too soon.

A few hours later, I start to speak to the gang members about what they are seeing when from the corner of my eye I notice movement at the front door. "Keep watching how your lives are going to be ..." Then I stop when I see him, "Matt, what are you doing here?" Is he stupid coming in like this knowing he is banned from this place?

"I should ask you what the hell you're doing here. And Logan, Jack, Chloe, what the hell is going on?" They had transformed back into their human form.

"You're not supposed to be here either." Jack heads towards his brother.

"Yeah, you reckon I'm going to listen to our parents and their stupid rules. These people here have more respect for me than my own family."

"Matt don't be so gullible, these people are only using you to get to us. It's your family who loves you, we will always have your back."

I feel a movement before I see him charging towards Jack and Matt, Donovan has woken from the spell. "Get away Jacky, leave your brother alone. He's one of us now." Matt's face shows how pleased he is, which makes me worry he has actually been brainwashed by this gang.

I'm also stunned because it's only been three hours since I cast the spell and it's already worn off for Donovan. Maybe the tweaking to make the spell affect shorter so they remember has made it too short. This is a huge problem because if any of the other members come out of it, we're in trouble.

But there is more trouble about to happen ...

Jack turns from Matt to see Donovan about to throw a hit so he ducks sideways. Matt doesn't see Donovan's fist coming.

I burst into action, pulling Donovan onto the floor and yelling at everyone to help me get Matt out of here. "Logan, call an ambulance." Before I leave the room, I cast another paralysing spell onto Donovan. This should keep him down for a few more hours.

TWENTY-ONE

Edward
A Close Call

LOGAN WALKS into the lounge after being with Jack at the hospital. He looks shattered.

"Here sit down, I'll get you a drink."

"Thanks Mum, I'm ok. Let me sit for a minute." She heads to the kitchen anyway.

"So how is he?" asks Dad.

"Umm, apparently Donovan's fist hit him square on the chin, which is bad enough but when he fell hitting the side of his head, his brain went into a frenzy and hit against this skull causing concussion. The surgery on his chin seems to have worked, but he hasn't woken up yet. The doctors say the concussion is the cause, they are keeping him sedated."

I am sitting on the edge of the lounge closest to Logan, "I'm so sorry. How is Jack? I've spoken to Noel and Hannah, they are beyond angry." As much as Matt has caused all sorts of trouble, does he really need to be in this position?

He looks at me, his eyes distraught and full of sorrow, "Jack is worried Matt may not recover fully, or at all. He's feels guilty for moving sideways leaving Matt so exposed."

Sally has walked in and heard, "That's not true, this is on Donovan. Jack was only looking after himself, he has nothing to feel guilty about." She hands me a glass of water.

"But he will blame himself if Matt doesn't pull through." Logan begins to shudder with sobs, "he ... he doesn't deserve this. As much as he is painful, he doesn't deserve to die." Sally runs over and hugs him, reassuring him Matt will be fine. "Stop thinking like that, Matt is young, he will pull through."

Sally is distraught, her body shaking, she shudders as she continues, "Enough of this silly talk, Matt will pull through, we all have to believe he will." She let's go of me and stands, "It could have been you in that hospital bed, it is only due to luck you are ok. She begins to cry. I walk towards her and she falls into my arms.

I feel her calming and say with heaviness, "Sally, you're right, we don't know what will happen to Matt but we need to have faith he will pull through." Sally's head drops onto my chest as she keeps quietly crying. I do hope Matt will be ok because the pain it will cause if he doesn't will be a catastrophe, not only for Noel, Hannah and Jack, but for Donovan as well."

TWO WEEKS later I'm with Ester, Leafia and other committee members at the Alliance house. We are seated at the table again.

"Well, it seems we avoided a disaster at the gang headquarters. Well done Edward for your quick thinking and getting everyone to safety. And for making sure Donovan wasn't going to cause more trouble by paralysing him again."

"Thanks Ester, running on pure adrenalin, my body and mind were working overtime. It felt like hours but I know it was only a few minutes. Logan calling the ambulance and them turning up quickly was a great help. Matt is recovering well, but he will be in hospital for another few weeks. It was touch and go for the first week, we were all extremely worried. I can't tell you how I felt for Noel and Hannah. Jack was a mess, we kept a close eye on him too." The others mutter and whisper while nodding as well. "But Hannah has been using her healing skills on her son, we are all sure this will help him to fully recover. And we're all hoping the knock on the head has put some sense into him."

"Yes, Hannah does have a healing touch, Matt is a lucky boy. By the time we arrived at the headquarters in the early hours, some of the members had come out of the spell. Two of them, the leaders, were trying to wake the others up. We were cautious to sneak in and began performing the memory spell. We're sorry about the timing of the paralysing spell, Edward, we have fixed that glitch."

"That's smart, thanks Leafia. With Donovan coming out of it so early, anything could have happened. Our magic was definitely exposed there for a bit." We all mutter in agreement knowing this was yet another close call.

We continue discussing how we can help the Sterling family and assist them even further when Matt returns home. Leafia tells us about the goblin's plan to check all of our most used spells and make sure they work as they should. Ester announces an upgrade of magical studies to discuss how to handle mishaps like spells not going the distance and how to avoid any other close calls from happening. Exposing our magic like we did this time was beyond dangerous.

The meeting finishes with me feeling drained after what was an eventful month, and not in a good way. I was looking forward to being at home with Sally and Logan. I'm grateful nothing happened to Logan, Jack or Chloe, or me for that matter, but what happened to Matt was weighing heavy on my mind. I was responsible for everyone's safety that night, but who was to know that Matt would turn up and cause such chaos. Had he not been so stubborn and not gone against his parent's wishes, this could all have been avoided.

NOEL and I are sitting by the pool, beers in hand. He is telling me how scared he was when Matt was in hospital. "Edward, what if he had not pulled through … honestly, it hurts to think about it. But I'm still angry with him for going against our wishes and heading down to the gang's head-quarters. And it just so happened to be the night you were all there."

I nod at the irony of Matt turning up, it was definitely a case of being 'at the wrong place at the wrong time'. Sally and Hannah join us placing snacks on the table. "Had he listened to you and Hannah he would not have spent the last three weeks in hospital. I'm glad to see Matt is doing better. I know how relieved you both are."

"Thanks, Edward. It's mainly his doing, I have found my healing doesn't help him as much as it would if he wasn't my child. It's strange, my emotions limit my ability to heal him, which has been frustrating."

"Wow, that is strange. You would think your powers

would work better on someone you are related to. Or, in any case, work the same as for everyone else."

"That's not the case, Sally. Being so close to someone places my emotions ahead of the healing. It's like me loving my boys too much means my healing powers are partially blocked by the emotions I feel for them."

There is silence for a minute as we take in this information. "It's wrong, you have healing powers for a reason, they should work on everyone. This is something we should bring up at the next meeting, Edward."

"I have spoken to Ester about this, Sally. We can try to discuss it as you say, but according to Ester it is an ancient law to stop any healer from using their powers to the detriment of others. It was a measure put in place to stop healers from healing only their own family members to increase their power within the magical community."

I bow my head in disgust at such a stupid law and look up to see Sally angered by this. "How absolutely ridiculous, healers like you have compassion for all, not just your families. No, this definitely needs more discussion. Edward, note this down as the first course of business for the next meeting. And I do think modern magicals would not use their healing powers to advance their standing in our community."

I think about The Five group of magicals who wanted me out of the magical society and wonder whether they would use their healing powers, if they have any, to make their position stronger. I have a feeling they would. Making a mental note to add this to the agenda with a small caveat to protect all of us, I say as calmly as I am able, "Will do Sally, now sit down before your head explodes, being this angry tonight won't help the law to be changed."

Hannah pours her a glass of white wine, she sits and

takes a long slug, her face changing from angry red to Sally-pale within seconds.

"Thanks Edward. Whatever we can do to change this law, we should. With Leafia checking many of our spells, maybe we can all help her to revoke this one." She raises her glass, "To Matt making a full recovery, those bullies getting what they deserve, and us magicals being able to do good without endangering our secret."

"Hear, Hear," we all say as we settle into a pleasant evening of discussing anything but that fateful night.

As we drive home, Sally asks me what I think about that law.

"It was probably necessary at the time it was put in place, but we don't need it if it stops healers from doing their work. It did make me think of The Five and the likes of anyone who has grudges like they did, how such a law would benefit them. If the law is revoked, then they could use it in their favour."

Sally is quiet for a minute, shuffles in the car seat to look towards me, "Oh, you're right. We can't let that happen."

"Don't worry, I've already added a note to the agenda for our next meeting, we will need a caveat to prevent any wrongdoing from those who are against us."

She slips back into her seat sighing and we remain with our own thoughts the rest of the way home.

TWENTY-TWO

Logan
Our Magic is Safe

WE'VE NEVER SEEN the A-Alliance house so full of magicals as dad, mum and I walk out to the meadow. There are magicals from all over the world here to celebrate with us all the fact our magical laws have been changed and our spells are now tighter than ever. Their performance will not be questioned for a long time.

Our committee members, Leafia and her team of goblins, along with all the overseas committee members had formed a special taskforce to oversee these changes. The law stopping healers from helping their own family members was revoked and another law stating only in certain circumstances would such measures be implemented. There were terms like, 'if a healer is seen to be mentally unstable ...', 'members of such family were known to seek revenge ...' 'a healer is using this gift to gain more personal power ... and so on.

Every magical had been sent details of how to update their powers of certain spells, the ones we all used on a regular basis, especially the paralysing and memory spells. Our own special powers were not touched as they worked within us, they were a part of us. Our powers are what makes us special and unique, each of us using them in our own way.

Ester and Leafia greet us as we head to where they are seated, at a long table for all the committee members, there were six of these tables all adorned with food, drink and delicacies brought from other countries. It is a feast like I've never seen before. I don't know where to start.

It doesn't take me long to fill my plate and go to sit with Chloe and Jack. They're sitting at a table full of kids our age and I look forward to talking to the many from overseas.

"Jack, I didn't see your parents?"

"No, they decided to stay home with Matt. Dad had told Mum to come with me, but she wanted to stay home, keep them company."

"That's a pity, they put in a lot of work to help change that law, they should be here celebrating."

"Yeah, probably, but Matt is still fragile, so, there you go."

Matt's recovery has been slow, but Hannah will be able to help him more now with the law changed. We're all hoping he behaves once he has recovered with his dad promising to ground him for life if he doesn't change his ways.

Soon, Ester and Leafia are both on stage now welcoming us all. Two members of each committee are on stage with them, phones are snapping photos like crazy. A journalist from our magical society online news portal is here too, this will be broadcast to all magicals the world over and we feel honoured to be hosting this huge event.

There are congratulations, special award ribbons, and special mentions of all the members who contributed the many hours of work that had gone into all of this. Leafia and her team are acknowledged and the cheers are deafening when Ester announces this and gives Leafia a bunch of flowers bigger than her and an award ribbon. It takes three goblins to hold the flowers. Laughter rings out from all of us as they struggle to hold them.

The celebrations continue with speeches from select members of our committee and others from overseas. This is when the three of us tune out and talk about what's happening in our lives.

We include the overseas kids who are sitting near us, a boy from Korea whose father was head of their committee, twin girls from England whose mother is head of that committee. Next to me is a young girl from Argentina, who had an interesting story to tell.

"My name is Delfina, I started my secondary level this year." We take it she means high school. "My parents are both in parliament so they are well known in Argentina. My father is in the Ministry of Health, my mother is in Foreign Affairs. I attend a special school for children of parliamentarians, which makes me feel safe."

"I thought Argentina was a safe country?"

"Generally, it is, Logan. But with being magical as well as the only daughter of a well-known couple, there are those who would do us harm. I board at my school and go home for holidays, both of which are safe havens for children like me. Our home is guarded 24/7."

I think about what she is telling us and am glad to live in a country like Australia where we have freedom and live in relative safety. Even though things have been ruined by bullies at times, mostly I feel safe living here. And now that our magical society has been strengthened against being found out, I feel safer still.

Once all the formalities are over, we all mingle talk to others. The twin girls who were sitting with us introduce me to their friends who also live in London. "Well, you need to look us up when you arrive. Here, let's exchange details so you can call us then we can all hang out. Is this a working holiday?"

I answer the tallest of the two boys, long hair dangling down his back, a semblance of a beard growing but sparse due to being him being fair. For the life of me I can't remember his name until I look at his details on my phone later, Edward, same as dad, how could I forget that? "Call me Eddie," he had said but I hadn't heard over all the commotion. Between the music and everyone talking, it was hard to hear anything. "I will need to work if I'm staying for a year."

"Not a problem, we'll help you with that too. My dad owns pubs, can you pull a beer?"

"Ha, no, but I'm sure I can learn."

"Of course, I'll teach you," Eddie laughs.

We talk till late, with Eddie and the twins introducing us to many of their other friends. With Europe being close to England, they knew people from all over. Jack and I are happy to be making friends before we are even on holiday, this will give us a boost once we arrive in London.

"Hey guys, it's been a great night, but I'm off home. Nice meeting you all and I look forward to seeing you soon." There are nods and thanks all round.

Chloe takes Jack's arm, "Come on, I'll walk you out."

She is back a few minutes later. "What was that all about, did Jack need an escort?"

"Oh, Logan, didn't you notice Jack wasn't himself tonight? I had wanted to ask him how things are at home but didn't want to say anything in front of all these people."

"I get it, he was quieter than usual."

"Yeah, he said things had improved with Matt being more responsible now, he seemed to be showing some remorse. But, you know, I still wouldn't trust him, he could easily go back to that gang and ruin his life."

"Maybe. We just have to wait and see. Although, this was a big scare for him, and he sees how it's ruined Donovan's life, he'll probably go to gaol again."

"I guess so, but he is a person who only thinks of himself. Remember Jack telling us how he does as he pleases without consideration for anyone else?"

"Yeah, I do. Chloe, I know you worry about Jack and Manuel, but they handled themselves well, those bullies were shocked how they fought back. If Matt goes off the rails again, we'll all be behind Jack, his family and, of course, Manuel." She calms herself with a sigh but I too am worried about Matt and what he will do once he's better.

We head to where our parents are at the committee table and sit listening to them talk about how well things have gone. Everyone is pleased with the work Leafia and her team put into fixing the spells, everyone giving a collective sigh of relief knowing the spells will all work as they should.

They will need to because that gang hasn't disappeared and even if Donovan isn't around, the gang will still target us.

TWENTY-THREE

Jack
  Formal is Here

SCHOOL IS COMPLETE FOR ME, Logan, Manuel and Aaron. We've already done our own celebrating but now we've been roped into helping the school committee organising our end of year formal. Not that I mind, I enjoy pitching in and making sure this party will be awesome. It is also taking my mind off what happened to Matt, he's home now but has a lot more recovering to do. *Look at me feeling sorry for my half-wit brother.*

The four of us are helping with arranging the tables and chairs while others are putting up decorations. The committee decided on a colour theme, so gold is everywhere, even the chairs have been covered in gold velvet. I think it's a sick idea but the boys aren't so sure.

"Feels like I've fallen into a vat of molten gold, this is too much."

"Oh come one, Aaron. Embrace your inner jewel thief and come dressed as one."

"Not likely, Jack. I might wear a gold tie, that's my limit."

I scoff and keep placing chairs where they're needed and decide I might come dressed as a jewel thief. Hmm, will have to look into what that looks like.

"Wow, this is so dope."

"What is Logan."

"The police have charged Donovan Schmidt with assault. He's going back to prison, this time for five years." He shows us his phone and we all read the news article.

Police have charged Donovan Schmidt, a known gang member, with assault after he allegedly hit a student from Redman High. This, along with other offences means he may receive a five-year sentence …

"He *may* go back to prison, Logan. Although, I can't imagine that he won't, with all the evidence against him. About time, too, I was pissed about what happened to my brother. You know he's still struggling, his head is feeling fuzzy even after weeks of being home."

"That's sad, I hope Matt isn't taking it out on you, Jack. And the gang members won't be too pleased to see Donovan back in prison."

"Let's hope they don't cause any more trouble, Manuel. And I wonder if they really care, they're all out to look after themselves. And Matt, he's ok towards me now, we're getting on because he's so subdued. I hope it lasts. Although there is a part of me that thinks he deserves all of this."

Logan and Aaron nod with Aaron adding, "He has been a jerk towards you Jack. To all of us actually, so I don't blame you feeling like that."

We continue talking about this incredible news about

Donovan's prison sentence and soon we have finished setting up. I go and tell the committee members we're leaving, "Do you need us back here any earlier?"

"No thanks, Jack. We'll take it from here, you guys come at seven when the formal starts."

I thank the girl who answered but I don't remember her name. She is the one who suggested the gold theme.

MATT WALKS into my room as I'm putting on my finishing touches. "What the hell are you wearing? What's with the stripes and all the gold?"

Since he's been home and more chilled I've allowed him into my room as long as he doesn't touch anything. "I'm a jewel thief, look here's my mask." I show him the black cat eye mask that I can hold onto my face. "Aren't the stripes obvious? Jewel thieves wear stripes but don't ask me why? I guess it has something to do with what they wear in gaol when they're caught. The gold jewellery is because our theme is the colour gold."

"Your formal has a theme? I didn't know that was a thing."

"According to the organising committee it is. You look better, how are you feeling?"

Matt sits on the end of my bed and sighs, "Still feeling a bit vanilla, you know, weak and my head is fuzzy. Going back to school hasn't helped, but then we finish in two weeks, so who cares."

"Even though Donovan's punch didn't hit you square on, you still copped a fair whack of it. Be patient, as Mum says, time will heal."

"Guess so. Her healing powers are helping now the new

law has been passed. It's still a slow process, but I feel better every time she does some healing on me."

I nod my head so he knows I like what is happening with his recovery as I'm brushing down my black suit with the lint roller and turn towards him, "I think I'm done."

"Now you've told me what your costume is, I can see you're a thief. Enjoy the evening, bro." I watch as he staggers out of my room, more like an old man than a seventeen-year-old boy. I do hope his recovery speeds up, with summer holidays coming up he won't want to be unwell.

I'M in the car with dad heading to pick up Manuel, he's my date. When I see him walk out in a gold jacket with shawl lapels, black formal pants and shiny AF shoes, I fall in love with him all over again. He has nailed tonight's theme.

"Hi and thanks Mr Sterling, my parents were busy tonight," he greets us as he sits in the car next to me.

I know he is lying but don't comment, his parents are not happy about us and avoid talking to their son as much as possible. I simply say, "You look fabulous," giving him a peck on the cheek.

Dad drops us at the venue. "Enjoy yourselves, let me know if you need a lift home."

"Thanks, but should be all good, we're planning a long night." I take hold of Manuel's hand and we walk in to see the others have already arrived.

"Manuel. Jack. Look at you two." Chloe comes up and kisses both our cheeks.

"Thanks, but everyone has made an effort. Logan, loving your gold hat and cane. And Tahlia, wow, that is some shimmery dress." She looks fabulous in a tight-fitting sheath dress with a long V-neck hugging her boobs and hips.

"Jack, don't forget Chloe and Aaron, stunninggggg!" Chloe has a dress similar in style to Tahlia but with a scoop neckline and not as much shimmer. Aaron, true to what he had said, was in a black suit, white shirt and gold tie.

We all laugh at Manuel waving his hand showing us how impressed he is. But he's right, everyone is in their best gold-themed outfits, even our teachers look great.

After more greetings and air kisses, our principal asks us to all stand on the dance floor. Once we are all quiet, he starts, "Welcome all of you to your end of year formal, the end of your primary and secondary years. Congratulations on coming this far and myself and your teachers wish you all the best for your futures. Congratulations too to the committee members on this fabulous venue, the decorations are magnificent. Now please find your seats as dinner will be served, we'll have more speeches later."

The evening flows with us chatting, boisterous laughter and a lot of dancing. We're also fuelled by a sneaky flask of vodka Aaron snuck in. "How did you get away with that?"

"Ah Jack, I have my methods," he snickers, "Not to be shared with anyone."

More laughter rings out as we dance, have more sneaky drinks and before we know it, our formal ends. Our future is ahead of us.

We're staggering out of the venue wondering what do to next when Logan announces, "Hey everyone, Ailsa texted, she's at The Arms. Let's go." We're all happy to keep this party going.

TWENTY-FOUR

Logan
   Ailsa's Surprise

THE GLENNDALE ARMS is not too far from the venue so we all walk to the pub. Tahlia and Georgia have changed into flats and Chloe was already in flat shoes, she had blinged them for the event. It was nice not having them whinging about sore feet and keeping up with us boys.

We head to our usual spot at the back and find Ailsa ... with Travis. "Put your eyes back in your head Logan. Yes, we're dating. I told you Kendric wasn't treating Ailsa right."

"Umm ... Hi, you two." I am shocked and will talk to Als later about what happened with Kendric. Als looks at me knowing I will have more to say later.

"Stunning guys, all looking awesome tonight. Loving all this gold." Als waves her hand up and down impressed by our outfits.

We settle ourselves in and I ask, "Ok, I'm headed to the bar, who wants what?" After hearing what everyone wants to drink I'm at the bar ordering when Travis comes up next to me.

"Ailsa will tell you more but you had better get used to having me around more, we're officially dating."

With tray in hand, I say, "I'm happy for you bro. As long as Als is happy, then it's fine by me. I don't have anything against you, you were being a dick that night, that's all. I didn't know Kendric any better than you, but he didn't deserve you trying to muscle in on Als."

"Yeah, I get that but I was sloshed and can be full of myself when I'm like that. Plus, I was taken by your friend."

"You're forgiven and Als is worth it. Here's your beer." Handing him a bottle, he smiles. I am pleased we're ok, Travis isn't all bad.

It's a busy Friday night and the band is pumping out tunes from rock to metal anthems, and later, ballads. When Als and Travis come off the dance floor and he heads to the bathroom, I ask her what happened.

"Kendric wasn't the person I hoped he'd be. Apart from being jealous, which was stifling, he wanted to control what I did, where I went and, this is the worst part, what I wore. We only lasted a few months. I was attracted to Travis from that first night, we started dating while I was still with Kendric. He lost it when he found out but Travis handled the situation like a gentleman and protected me. And I'm with a magical. I really am part of your society now. He's the one Logan, if you know, you know."

"Wow, that's a big call, Als. And what are you talking about, you've always been a part of us. Anyway, Travis did say on that night Kendric wasn't treating you right, so I'm happy for you both. Travis is a good guy, he treated me well when we first met at the Alliance house."

"Ah, yes, he mentioned he met you when you were younger and saw you often at the house."

"Yeah, we did see each other but I wouldn't call us friends."

We settle into a rhythm of chatting, drinking and dancing. Others come from the formal and the pub is at capacity by the early morning. The atmosphere is great, all of us talk about our hopes for the future and where to next. Jack, Manuel and I have already started to plan our gap year and even though I asked Tahlia to come along for maybe a month, she said she would rather stay home and prepare for Year 12. "We can see each via video anytime," she had said.

When the pub closes, some of us head to the park, ready to chill out before heading home. Jack and Manuel hold each other up, Georgia and Aaron had hooked up at the pub and were continuing their face-fest at the park table. Tahlia is sitting on my lap talking about Als. "She looks happy. Happier than when she was with the other guy." Als and Travis had left us and I know they were headed to his place.

"You noticed she wasn't happy with Kendric?"

"Yes, didn't you? She wasn't herself around Kendric, he had some type of weird obsession with her."

Thinking back I see that now. "Things have worked out for the better, good on them." I place my finger under her chin and turn her towards me, "Just like they have for us." I kiss her gently at first, then passion takes over. I suggest we go and find a quiet spot somewhere.

"My mum isn't home, let's go to my place." No one could wipe the huge smile off my face as I order us an Uber.

I WORK my butt off to earn more money for my trip and before I know it, the three of us boys are at the airport heading to Europe. I had said goodbye to Tahlia the night before, we shared the night together. She had shed a tear or two, which I found sweet and even though I was going to miss her, I was pumped to be going away for a whole year.

Us boys weren't spending the whole time together, Jack and Manuel had a different agenda to mine, so for much of the trip I was going solo. This was both intimidating and amazing at the same time. Although, we had the names of the magicals we met at the last event and I'm looking forward to learn how to pull a beer. I have to work for some of this holiday if I am going to afford a whole year.

Jack, Manuel and I are sitting at the Qantas gate, our flight is leaving in thirty minutes. We had talked all the way here about the things we were looking forward to and are still talking when our departure is announced.

For Jack and me, this was our first overseas trip. Manuel had been back to South America with his family a few times. He had told us what to expect. What hit me the most was how crammed in we were in the narrow seats, now I know how a sardine feels. Having walked through business class, one day I hope to travel like that, if not first.

Thirty-two hours later we land in London. We found cheap flights but the compromise is more stops and longer flying time to get to your destination. I'm feeling jaded from lack of sleep and too much alcohol, but as we collect our bags, excitement kicks in. This is going to be extra, the trip of a lifetime.

TWENTY-FIVE

Logan
 Eight Years Fly By

I'M SITTING on Tahlia's bed, she is next to me crying. After my return from the gap year trip, where I had done a lot of growing up, Tahlia and I had resumed seeing each other. We kept in touch often while I was away, but halfway through the trip, I started seeing her as a naïve young girl, not at all like the women I had met during my travels. I loved her, she was my first love after all, but things had changed for me.

I have my arm around her shoulder letting her cry it out. I've been here for an hour and am happy to stay as long as she needs me.

"I'm fine now," she says sniffing, "you can go."

"I can stay if you like, there's no hurry."

"Logan, I can't be your friend right now. Maybe in future, but not when you've told me what you have. I'm happy you found who you are on this trip, and maybe one day I need to do something like that for myself, for now, please go."

I turn and place both arms around her shoulders, kissing her deeply. "You're special Tahlia, don't forget that. You and I had a great thing going, I will always cherish what we had." As she begins to cry again, I hug her as tears begin to spill from my eyes too.

Driving home, the heaviness in my body takes me by surprise, I didn't think it would be so hard to break up our relationship. It all sounded so easy in my head while I was away, but as it took me two months before I could actually break up with her, my feelings for her were still there, just not as strong as they were. I hope we can remain friends in the future like she said.

To my disappointment, that was the last time I saw Tahlia, our lives going in different directions.

MY TIME at university was some of the best times of my life. The workload was overwhelming at first, but once I was used to uni life, I was better able to handle my business degree. I worked in dad's business while studying and planned to work my way up. I found I enjoyed working in construction but after finishing my degree, I felt something was missing.

Travel became a staple in my life, a trip a year to London, one of my favourite destinations. From there it was easy to travel throughout Europe and I worked in some places making it possible to stay longer depending on university holidays. Many of the magicals I'd met back at the celebration we had back home became firm friends, we kept in touch regularly.

The feeling something was missing stayed with me,

though. I found myself drawn to admiring the architecture of the many cities I visited, which is where the initial idea of studying to be an architect started.

After my longest trip away from home, which was two years, I decided to stay put for a bit because a few of my friends were talking marriage. It was to be a few years before I headed back to London to realise my dream of becoming an architect.

During this time, I ran into Donovan, he had been out of gaol for some years and was reformed. "I saw how my life was heading and didn't want to go back to prison, it was hell in there," he had told me. "And those gang members, supposed to be my friends ... never heard from any of them the whole time I was in prison. So much for protection and the gang code."

"They had a code?"

"Yeah, an unwritten rule that if any of us was in trouble, they'd have our back. Obviously, no one enforced it, hey?"

He was working as a labourer and had a son, he seemed happier than I had ever seen him. I told him I was pleased to see him as a better version of the person I once knew and gave him credit for doing so.

He continued to tell me how he avoided any of the gang members and even apologised for being such an idiot towards me and the other geeks. "I'm sorry to have hurt you and Jack. And then, of course, Matt. That got me into so much more trouble. There was no need to become so violent."

This was something so unexpected I hadn't reacted at first, then put my hand out to shake his, "Thanks Donovan, I'll be glad to pass your apology to any of the others I see," I had finally replied.

.   .   .

A SEPTEMBER WEDDING

September rolls around and it's eight years since our return from our gap-year trip. Jack and Manuel moved in with each other soon after we arrived home as Manuel couldn't fathom the reason why his parents wouldn't accept him being gay. He has two other siblings who can give them grandkids and whatever else heterosexual couples give, why did they insist he be the same as his brother and sister?

This is now in the past and Manuel has not spoken to his family since. All of their friends can't believe what has happened, but he had explained his parents were stuck in a time warp and were narrow minded. His sister sometimes called him to make sure he's doing ok and she probably reported back to his parents, why else would she call? But none of this matters now because they are getting married and I'm their best man. Aaron is the other witness.

Both Aaron and I were surprised Jack hadn't picked Matt as his best man, but he did explain his brother being a dick for so many years and joining that gang did muddy the waters between them. The gang is now a thing of the past for Matt, the smartest move he ever made. Jack and he speak, sometimes seeing each other but Matt continues with the sibling rivalry occasionally, this will never change.

The Wedding Day is here and unfortunately it's raining as we're getting dressed at Jack and Manuel's place, a chic terrace they managed to buy in Surry Hills. Well, it's chic now, but it was a knockdown when they bought it. "We're screwed for life," Jack had laughed, "this mortgage is going to kill us."

I always doubted they were going to have a problem paying it, with Manuel being a lawyer and Jack a successful actor and singer, they managed. Yes, Manuel did finally decide what he wanted to do, he was the go-to lawyer for many gay people who found themselves in trouble.

Well the rain turned out not to be an issue, as the ceremony has been moved indoors. I stand next to Jack, who is resplendent in a replica gold jacket Manuel wore to our formal, and Manuel is dressed in a more subdued black suit with a shirt in a matching gold. Aaron is standing next to Manuel. The celebrant is a friend of theirs and when they say their vows, us friends and some loved ones, are all wiping tears away.

After the obligatory photos, we head to the reception at the same venue our formal was held, which was the reason Jack had decided on the jacket, he wanted the retro style because it held lovely memories for him.

They had booked the smallest room and the sun was out now so the when the cars pulled up outside the venue, we just had to scoot around the puddles that hadn't dried up yet.

An intimate wedding, Als and Travis were there along with Georgia and her current boyfriend and Chloe. She and Arron are next to be married in early December. There were also Jack's acting friends and Manuel's work colleagues, but we numbered no more than forty. For me, it was a perfect amount of people, just enough to have a party.

Jack and Manuel danced for the first time as a married couple to a recording of a song Jack had written. We were all smitten and felt the love they had for each other. This was a touching part of the reception, Manuel had tears dripping down his face for the whole dance.

Als comes up to me asking me to dance and I look around for Travis. "He's gone outside for some air, and something else I imagine."

"He's calming himself down, right?" I know about

Travis feeling overwhelmed when he's around too many people, especially ones he doesn't know. Even though he seemed confident, Travis had a social phobia. He had hidden it well, but he feels better now we all know, he feels safe around us. I turn down the dance and she sits next to me agreeing it's easier to talk away from the dance floor.

"So, I ran into Tahlia last week, she says hi."

"Thanks, how is she?" I hadn't seen her since we broke up, she had moved to the city and worked in marketing.

"Good, she enjoys her work and loves living in the city. Walks to work, has everything she needs around her, living a good life. Her mother passed, did you hear?"

"No, I didn't that's sad. I'll send her a message or maybe call her."

"I suppose you could but it was a few years ago now, an aggressive form of cancer. Happened quickly."

"That's so sad. Well, if I ever run into her, I'll say something." I say this but somehow doubt it will ever happen.

"What about you, no one on the horizon?"

"Since finishing my degree and working my way up in my dad's business, I've decided to go back and study. I want to be an architect." I had an inkling I wanted to return to study when I finished my business degree but wasn't sure what I wanted to do at the time.

"Good for you."

"Yeah, in London. I've been accepted at UCL, the University College London. I went to see the campus on my trip last year and met someone while I was there."

Ailsa's face lights up, "You're moving to London, how fabulous. You did say how much you liked it the first time you went. That wonderful gap year that changed your life. So, spill, details please."

"Elizabeth Dobey, she's an English major and but

everyone knows her as Liz. We met at the pub near the campus, she works for a publishing company in the area." I pull out my phone and show Als a photo.

Taking it from my hand, she takes a good long look. "An English rose complexion, red curls and she looks smitten by you. Well done *you*." She emphasises her last word, smiling at me with approval.

Taking my phone back, "We have a lot in common, our love of sport, enjoy the same music and food, and my Grandmother Elizabeth is pleased to have a namesake. They have met on our video chats. Liz took my breath away when I saw her standing at the bar, her green eyes focused on me and I couldn't stop staring back. Luckily she didn't hate me staring and joined me at my table. I was on my own having only been in London a week."

Als grabs me and gives me a hug, "I'm pleased for you ..." She is about to say more when Travis joins us.

"It's raining again so I came back in. What's with the smiles on your faces." Als explains why and Travis slaps me on the back, "Well done, bro."

Jack and Manuel leave soon after, heading straight for the airport for their honeymoon in New York. Manuel has friends there and they will be celebrating with them for two weeks before heading to Hawaii to relax on one of the smaller islands. I feel happy for them but am sad his family is missing out on how happy he is, I don't understand people who won't change their views, not even for their own son. I couldn't imagine my parents doing something like that to me. For that I'm grateful.

AFTER SAYING goodbye and Merry Christmas to my family, I'm at the airport at the same gate where I boarded my gap year flight. I will spend Christmas Day with Liz and her family. My future now lies in what happens in London, another adventure ahead of me.

THE END

ACKNOWLEDGMENTS

When I wrote Book One, *Edward's Cat. A Magical Tale of Edward, his Twin and a Cat.*, of this magical story I didn't know there was more to come. Book Two, *Edward's Cat. The Rise of the Kittens. And a Dog.*, is also available to buy. Now there is Book Three, *Edward's Cat. Three Cats, a Magical Legacy. And a Dog.*, the trilogy is complete. At this stage, I see a trilogy, but who knows? Will there be more to the magicals stories?

The idea for Edward's story started as a writing prompt for one of my writing groups, Write on Water. It is thanks to the other authors in that group that this story is now published. I thank you, especially those who helped with reading and editing, your suggested changes were invaluable. A big thank you to my beta readers as well who helped me polish the three stories in this trilogy.

As always, thanks to my colleague and friend, Mark Drolc, for designing my book covers. You are patient, put up with my changes, and always enhance my ideas. Even when things become too busy, you always find time to design my covers. A huge thanks to you, Mark.

Each Edward's Cat story is a novella, longer than a short story but not quite a novel. This doesn't make it any easier to write, but no less enjoyable. My ideas keep coming and story ideas flow freely so I will keep writing as long as my readers are entertained by the stories I create.

Of course, thanks go to my family, my friends and my colleagues. A special shout out to my author friends, we all help each other to be the best we can be. Each and every one of you is behind me encouraging my creativity, and for this I'm grateful.

ABOUT THE AUTHOR

Maria has made a career of using words to communicate. Working at a TV station, her first paid job, nurtured Maria's love of words. A move to Sydney to study Communications gave her the opportunity to work with advertising & public relations agencies, corporate companies and newspapers. She has written PR, ads and newsletters for products from food to jewellery, fashion and interiors as well as garden and building products. When she is not writing corporate communications or as a Senior Reviewer for the online site, Weekend Notes, she works on her short stories and novels.

Her first published story, *The Studio* is a crime short story. *Xenure Station: A Billion Light Years,* is Maria's second short story. Both are available as eBooks online.

The Decision They Made, Maria's debut novel and her other books are available on her website – www.mariapfrino.com. Buy these books as eBooks or print. *Weaving Words,* an anthology Maria collaborated on, is also available as an audiobook. Maria contributed two short stories to this anthology along with eight other authors.

Along with several other authors, Maria helped to establish **Sydney Authors Inked,** a collective of self-published authors who do author and book talks. They discuss books, reading, publishing, and all book-related topics. This year they introduced an interview format - **In Conversation with Sydney Authors Inked,** where an author, traditionally or self-published, is interviewed. These talks are held at The Little Big House, Summer Hill, a beautiful space where events like the Sydney Authors Inked ones are held regularly. Anyone interested is welcome to attend, look out for tickets on Humanitix.